Murder at Canterbury Faire

Murder at Canterbury Faire

A Dr. Emily Goldman Mystery

Sharon Freeman Laborde

Cahaba Press
Eureka Springs
2014

Cahaba Press
483 County Road 231
Eureka Springs, AR 72631
USA
www.cahabapress.com

This is a work of fiction. The characters, names, incidents, dialogue and plot are the product of the author's imagination.

Quotes from the *Canterbury Tales* are from *Canterbury Tales Rendered into Modern English* by J.U. Nicolson. Garden City Publishing Co., Inc. New York. 1934

Cover Image: *The Story of the Canterbury Pilgrims Retold from Chaucer* by F. J. Harvey Darton and illustrated by M.L. Kirk. 1914. Courtesy of karenswhimsy.com
Cover Design: Sharon Freeman Laborde and Penguin Graphics II, Eureka Springs, AR

First Edition 2014 by Cahaba Press

ISBN-10: 0615976387
ISBN-13: 9780615976389

For
Celeste and David Laborde

Grateful acknowledgment is made to my dear friends: Faye Knopf, Dr. Renée Norrell, Georgia "Peach" Holland and Sharon Gaydon for their friendship, suggestions and encouragement.

When April with his showers sweet with fruit
The drought of March has pierced unto the root
And bathed each vein with liquor that has power
To generate therein and sire the flower...
****
THE PROLOGUE OF THE CANTERBURY TALES
BY
GEOFFREY CHAUCER

Chapter I

At first all she could hear was the jingling of the tiny silver bells adorning the bridles of the horses; but as her eyes adjusted to the light, she could see the long line of pilgrims dressed in garments of medieval finery as they emerged from the mist. Their faces, cloaked against the early morning chill, were hidden as the fog swirled around the legs of the horses and the bodies of the riders. As the procession became clearer in the unearthly light, she recognized the host, Harry Bailey, as he led the travelers on their journey toward Canterbury Cathedral and the tomb of the blessed Saint Thomas à Becket. It seemed that he was about to speak, to perhaps encourage them to begin to tell their tales; but suddenly his face contorted in a hideous grimace and, clutching his chest, he fell from his horse onto the soft wet ground. Through the mist she could see him lying on his back, his eyes staring heavenward; and she began to scream.

She was breathing rapidly, and her heart was thumping in her chest as she threw off the bedcovers. Slowly she sat up on the edge of the bed searching for her slippers on the floor where she always placed them. "What a horrible dream," she said aloud, rubbing her eyes. She had been jolted awake, either from the shock of the nightmare or from the muffled sound she had made in her sleep as she saw the body hit the ground. The dream had been vivid with every detail so realistic she was still shaken. She suddenly realized the terrifying image she could see so clearly in her mind bore a marked resemblance to the new head of the English Department, Dr. Basil Bowen. She glanced at her alarm clock on her bedside table and had another shock.

Dr. Emily Goldman, Chaucer scholar and professor of English at Merryvale College, had actually overslept! She was going to be late for her eight o'clock class; and that was something that was unthinkable, something that had never occurred in her long tenure at the college. Why had she indulged in that additional glass of wine last night? She knew from experience that wine did not agree with her in the evening, and yet she had been tempted to indulge in just one more glass of a very nice Merlot.

Predictably she had awakened at 2:00 a.m. and had tossed and turned for at least an hour, maybe more, before drifting back to what must have been an uneasy sleep. When the dream jolted her awake, she realized she had been hitting the snooze button on her alarm and now she was running behind schedule. Totally disgusted with herself, her morning routine turned upside down, she prepared for the day as rapidly as possible.

"Maxwell of Dumfries, it seems to me you could at least bark when you hear the alarm," she chided her spoiled Scottie, known to one and all as Max.

His little black eyes looked up at her as if he was perfectly aware of what she was talking about; he cocked his head to one side and gave a short bark. "Too late now, little friend," she said, as she reached down and scratched his ears. Although she was in a rush, she made sure he had fresh water, his morning snack, and that the doggie door was open so he could go in and out to the back garden before she started to get ready for class. His short legs were a blur as his stocky little body

3

shot through the swinging door. I must hurry, she fretted.

The lapse that accounted for her second glass of wine at the home of her department head the previous evening, a rare indulgence, was understandable she thought, as she selected an outfit for the day from her neatly arranged closet. The faculty of the English Department had gathered to discuss preparations for the annual Canterbury Faire, an event that had put Merryvale College on the map and attracted a large crowd of enthusiastic spectators. Although planning for the Faire had been the focus of the meeting, Dr. Goldman sensed she was not the only one there who seemed to feel a bit uncomfortable in Dr. Bowen's home and that they were making very little headway in formulating plans for the yearly event. There was an undercurrent of discontent in the department, and momentarily a frown crossed her usually calm expression.

The faces of her dear colleagues did not radiate with their usual enthusiasm for the Faire either, and she felt a palpable tension in the usually genial atmosphere of the planning meeting. It would appear that the change in leadership that had occurred with the retirement of Dr. Stewart Stevens and the appointment of a new academic leader was still causing discontent in the department. Such a pity, she thought, since through the years they had all worked so happily together, but those happy days were in the past, not the present.

Unfortunately Dr. Bowen had ruffled more than a few feathers on his arrival, and as a consequence no one seemed to be at ease with the new department head. She couldn't quite put her finger on the problem, but the undercurrent of unhappiness and tension troubled her, and it may have been the feeling that things were not as they should be, more than the indulgence in a second glass of wine, which could account for her restless night.

Dr. Goldman's beloved English Department was the focus of both her personal and professional life, and there was very little that occurred in that academic world that didn't somehow come to her attention. As the meeting had progressed on the previous evening, she slowly sipped her glass of wine hoping to discover some way of diffusing the stress between the normally compatible members who had met at Dr. Basil Bowen's home. Perhaps a mistake had been made in not holding more informal meetings from the beginning of the year when Dr. Bowen first arrived, to get to know him better and to help him with his new duties; or perhaps it would have made no difference at all, she thought. Now all of the resentment that had built up during the first semester was coming out in the open. The meeting to discuss the Faire was the first time he had invited them to his house since he had taken over the department; and many felt he lacked the social sense to realize that this in itself was a slight to the faculty, just another example of his superior attitude.

As the meeting dragged on, Dr. Goldman, one of the chief organizers of the Faire in the past, had eventually grown weary of the controversy and suggested that they were all working at cross purposes since no one seemed to be able to agree on much of anything this year. After all, it was an event that had changed little over time, and all that was needed where planning was concerned was the delegation of responsibilities. She had pointed out to Dr. Bowen that the reenactment of Chaucer's *Prologue to the Canterbury Tales* was in no way an attempt to be a polished production. The Faire had always gone smoothly and there was really no reason to alter the plan that had been successful in previous years. Finally, weary of the endless discussion of details, she had bid them goodnight and returned to her home, still unsure what to do about the unease that had enveloped her of late and hoping she was wrong about her sense of impending trouble.

Dr. Emily Goldman, or simply Dr. Emily to her close associates, was a transplant to the Deep South; and she never failed to recognize the good fortune that had brought her to such an idyllic spot in the central part of Alabama. The small campus, shaded with huge old oaks and brick lined walks, may have been off the beaten path; but that had been one of the main attractions for her after growing up in the cold climate of Illinois and her years as a student and lecturer at the University of Chicago. After an initial period of culture shock, she had never regretted her decision to flee the brutal climate of the city that had been her birthplace and where she had made a name for herself as one of the finest Chaucer scholars and translators of Anglo-Saxon in the country.

She had been well liked and left behind many friends in Chicago and a smaller more intimate social circle, most in some way connected to the University. Her life was full and rich, but it wasn't enough after a failed relationship with a colleague in her department. The man had been a great disappointment to her; and coming so soon after the loss of both of her parents to illness and old age, she decided her best option was to make a fresh start somewhere else, somewhere far away from everything that reminded her of the unhappiness of the last few years. A change of scene was what she had needed, and at the time she thought it would only be for a short while, just until she had time to think and reflect. Her colleagues in the Department of Anglo-Saxon and Medieval Literature, awed by her brilliance, had always assumed she would move on at some time, probably to Yale or Harvard or one of the other Ivy League schools; so there was a sense of shock and surprise when she announced she planned to accept a position at a small Southern college that none of them had ever heard of, a college that was located in what they considered the hinterland.

No doubt she was suffering from some sort of crisis that she would soon be able to overcome: depression or a failed love affair, they speculated, a temporary case of nerves. Dr. Emily wasn't one to share her emotional life with her acquaintances, so most of her friends never realized her motivation for leaving. Only a few of her intimate friends knew about the emotional toll she had gone through. They had briefly tried to talk her out of it, of course, but she had persisted in her intention to leave what most scholars would consider a prime position in the academic world and settled into the small Victorian house at the edge of the Merryvale campus and had happily remained there for almost twenty-five years

On this early spring morning, although running behind schedule, she dressed carefully in the classic clothes she favored: the tartan skirt worn with her maroon cashmere sweater, the pearl necklace that had belonged to her mother, her sensible low-heeled pumps. April in Alabama was like every other month except July and August, unpredictable; and there was still a chill in the air. The light sweater would be perfect. Her short white curls caressed the edge of the black velvet beret that had become her trademark. She was rarely seen without it when the weather was cool.

She had an established routine of dressing each morning; but running late was certainly not part of her plan, and she felt rushed. Grabbing her briefcase, she locked the front door and headed across campus still annoyed with herself for sleeping through her alarm, still feeling out of sorts, and wondering what her students would think if she was not there waiting for them at the beginning of class.

Slightly out of breath, she rushed up the steps of Julia Tutwiler Hall, the venerable building that housed the English Department, becoming even more put out with herself with every minute that ticked by. She thought she might actually be able to hear them as the minute hand moved closer to the eight o'clock hour on her wrist watch, the one her dear mother had given her for a graduation present from undergraduate school all those years ago. Checking for a final time, she was relieved to see that she was going to make it at precisely eight and avoid being late—the UNTHINKABLE!

Suddenly she realized she would be so winded from her brisk walk and the climb to the second floor of the building that she would find it difficult to start the class with her usual obscure line from a long forgotten Anglo-Saxon narrative. Her mind was a blank—she couldn't think of a single quote! Her round cheeks were bright pink as she entered the classroom, and she noted unhappily that she was indeed the last one to enter the room.

The clock could be heard striking the hour from the tower on the Quad. Her students' upturned faces, many barely awake, but still looking forward to her lecture, looked at her expectantly. Dr. Goldman's class on Chaucer was one of the most popular courses in the department.

"Make no comments on my obvious tardiness! Let us take a moment to reflect in silence on the memory of Dr. Thomas Underwood of the University of Chicago, Professor Emeritus, on the anniversary of his death," she gasped. Turning her back abruptly, she picked up a dry-erase marker and wrote Dr. Underwood's name on the board, followed by a formidable list of academic credentials.

Looking at the class with a critical eye, she spoke with authority. "Will you please stand in honor of Dr.

Underwood?" It really wasn't a request—more like an order.

Amazingly, the entire group of English majors stood in silence; some even bowed their heads, although they had no idea who on earth Dr. Thomas Underwood could possibly be. Those who had not assumed a prayerful position in observance of this mysterious man shifted a little so they could catch each other's eyes. A few smiles were exchanged between the students who treasured Dr. Goldman's eccentricities. If nothing else, she kept them guessing.

After a prolonged moment of silence in which Dr. Emily was able to catch her breath and organize her thoughts, she felt she could go on with the lecture for the day.

"Let us begin with *The Prologue of The Canterbury Tales* by Geoffrey Chaucer," she trilled in her high melodic voice, and she was back in her element, all troubles of the previous night forgotten, and all thoughts of the upcoming Canterbury Faire put out of her mind. She was back in the more romantic past where most of her waking hours were normally spent. Ah, academia!

Then do folk long to go on pilgrimage,
And palmers to go seeking out strange strands,
To distant shrines well known in sundry lands.
****
THE PROLOGUE OF THE CANTERBURY TALES
BY
GEOFFREY CHAUCER

Chapter 2

After her lecture Dr. Emily ambled down the rather dim hallway of Tutwiler Hall toward the English Department office. Usually she waited until later in the day to check her departmental mail, finding the fewer contacts she made during the early morning hours with the other members of the department the more agreeable her day would be. Not that Dr. Emily was antisocial, far from it; she simply despised chitchat; and, besides, she was usually thinking about loftier matters. But on this morning, knowing that the department was all aflutter with preparation for the Canterbury Faire, she felt she would appear to be shirking her duty if she didn't at least check in with Dr.

Bowen's secretary, Glenda McWilliams, another new addition to the staff.

"Good morning, Glenda," Dr. Emily said over her shoulder as she checked for mail in her box. "Is Dr. Bowen in his office and available for a quick word? I still need to see him about a few things concerning the Faire. I've thought of several topics we failed to discuss last night at our meeting."

"Let me just give him a ring, Dr. Emily," Glenda replied, shoving the fashion magazine she had been perusing into a desk drawer. She was still new enough on the job to worry about things like that. Not that Dr. Emily would have cared if she had noticed. It was likely, however, that the new department head would have disapproved of anything that was not related to English Department business. He struck Dr. Emily as being the type who liked to micromanage everyone, but was not very successful. Actually, he was rather ineffectual, she thought.

Dr. Basil Bowen, Chairman of the English Department, had been welcomed with a great deal of enthusiasm when he was hired by Merryvale College to replace Dr. Stewart Stevens, whose tenure was long and whose retirement was well deserved. After an extensive search for a replacement, Dr. Bowen had come to Merryvale highly recommended by his former employer, a small liberal arts college in Virginia. He had the additional advantage of a degree from Oxford University, and as everyone knows Southerners are absolutely fascinated with the British. The more aristocratic the accent the better, and in that Dr. Bowen exceeded their expectations. It could be said that he was assured of the job the moment he opened his mouth.

He had been lured from his college in Virginia by the offer of the position of Chairman of the English Department, a highly sought-after tenure-track post. In the past Merryvale, always suspicious of outsiders, with the exception of Dr. Emily, had usually promoted from within the department after many years of observing professors and assuring themselves that whatever eccentricities they might possess were well within the bounds of decorum demanded by the college.

Dr. Emily had been the obvious candidate for department head considering her renown in academic circles and her seniority, but there had been several concerns about offering her the position. Everyone from the Dean of Academic Affairs to the Board of Trustees was well aware that she was not the slightest bit interested in the day-to-day administration of the department, but didn't want to hurt her feelings by passing over her in the selection process. It presented a real dilemma. Several members of the Board of Trustees expressed concern that Dr. Goldman might not be capable of running the department in an efficient manner since often her mind seemed to be somewhere else—no doubt with Geoffrey Chaucer, they joked.

Regrettably, a few members of the Board dug in their heels and let it be known, somewhat subtly of course, that they wanted a man in the position of department head. The Women's Movement in the South, sad to say, has had little impact on the *Good-Ole-Boy* network. Eventually, after a lot of squabbling and hoping that it would be refused, the position had been offered to her. Undoubtedly, their high regard for her had overcome their prejudices; but Dr. Goldman had shuddered in horror at the thought of being troubled with the problems of the present and the mundane business of pleasing students, parents, boards of accreditation and other nightmares. After expressing her appreciation, she declined the offer, making it clear that she was happy with teaching and doing her research and had no interest in the demands of administrative duties. The *Good-Ole-Boys* breathed a collective sigh of relief, sang her praises, and told one and all how lucky the college was to have a renowned scholar in the English Department.

Dr. Bowen, with his British accent and elegant manner, was their first choice after Dr. Goldman and eagerly accepted the position. On the surface it seemed things had worked out in a highly satisfactory manner. Dr. Bowen, after completing the first semester of his three-year conditional contract, had become a part of the small academic community of Merryvale College and, according to those willing to voice their opinion, seemed to be well on his way to making his own mark on the campus. He was liked by the students during those early days; and although possessing a degree of arrogance and the famous British reserve, he was accepted into the day-to-day life of the college, although he had gotten off on the wrong foot with a few members of his department. But these troubles had been more or less smoothed over, rather like the small ripples on a pond that slowly disperse after the occasional drop of rain hits the surface.

Dr. Bowen's wife, Elise, however, was a tsunami. First of all, she made it clear that she had no desire whatsoever to be there in a small town in central Alabama. Then she let everyone in the department know that she was a descendant of early settlers of Spotsylvania County, Virginia, who had been greatly impoverished by the War of Northern Aggression, as some in her state still referred to it. She was one of those pathetic women whose focus was on supposed long- ago injustices that her unfortunate ancestors had bequeathed to her: in other words, the loss of power and money or the money that could buy the power. Worse still, she had inherited from those ancestors of great fame, if only in her own mind, all of the least attractive genes in their pool. She loved to tell anyone who would listen how they did things in Spotsylvania County and how much better they did it. If ever there was an aristocratic bone in her ancestral fan chart, that particular DNA had certainly passed her by. But in all fairness, it was in character that she was deficient, rather than in appearance. She was remarkably lovely to look at, with golden blond hair, a flawless skin, and a figure both athletic and curvy.

"I hate to bother him at this early hour, Glenda, but I must go over some things with him since the Faire will be here before we turn around. Where does the time go?"

Glenda buzzed Dr. Bowen's office and told him Dr. Emily wanted a word. "He says he has time for a quick visit before his next meeting, Dr. Emily. I can't believe we have such a short time before the Faire and so much to do, but it'll be fun. I'm looking forward to it," Glenda said, rising from her desk and walking with her down the hall to Dr. Bowen's office. After giving a soft tap on the door, she opened it and stood back as Dr. Emily entered.

"Ah, Dr. Goldman, come in, come in," Dr. Bowen said. "Elise and I were just having a conversation about casting the characters in *The Canterbury Tales*. We seem to have failed to discuss that last night. I've told her I think it rather unsporting for the wife of the head of the department to get her pick of the parts. Your opinion on the matter will be appreciated, I'm sure. Do sit down."

Rather flustered, Dr. Emily quickly responded. "Oh dear, Glenda should have told me you were busy. So sorry to intrude, my dear," she said, looking at Elise and marveling at how the woman managed to look so elegant at such an early hour of the morning.

"Not to worry, I was just going," she replied but made no move to depart. Her long shapely legs were crossed, revealing a little more skin than Dr. Emily thought appropriate. She seemed nervous, swinging her leg in a rather agitated manner while looking at Dr. Emily with a critical eye.

"I've simply been trying to explain to Basil that I would be the only possible choice to play the part of the Prioress. I don't think that's an unreasonable request, do you Dr. Goldman?" Elise flashed a radiant smile in her direction; but there was a condescending note in her voice, as if to infer that Dr. Emily knew nothing about men or how to handle them.

Dr. Emily hesitated for a split second. "Dear me, I think you would make a lovely Prioress. We've always given the members of the department first choice in signing up for the parts. I don't see why you shouldn't have it if you wish. I suppose you would qualify as the spouse of a department member and doubt anyone would have any objections."

Dr. Emily knew that Dr. Stewart Steven's wife had always played the part of the Prioress, and wondered if she was still planning on taking part this year. This could be awkward, but she supposed things were bound to change now that Dr. Steven's was no longer head of the department. Dr. Emily had tried to keep an open mind about Elise Bowen, but was finding it increasingly difficult to do so. She couldn't help but think that although she was a beautiful woman she was shallow and petty.

"See, I told you Basil! Put my name down for the Prioress. I'll see you later at home." Her voice was petulant, but there was an underlying tone of assertiveness that made Dr. Emily wonder who really wore the pants in the family.

Basil sighed as Elise excused herself and flounced out the door in a trail of heavy perfume. "Sorry about that Dr. Goldman, she can be rather difficult at times. Once she has set her mind on something, it's rather hard to get her to see reason. I don't want anyone to think we play favorites here."

"Hum, of course," Dr. Emily murmured, not really knowing what to say.

"I'm ever so happy you stopped by this morning. The Faire is really taking on a life of its own. I don't know how you have managed through the years to pull it off, considering how little time you have allowed for the preparations." Basil's accent was like music to Dr. Emily's ears, but she thought his attitude rather condescending and couldn't help but notice the hint of criticism.

"Oh well. That's easily explained. You see, we've never thought of it as a polished production, and part of the charm and the fun has always been that it was basically unrehearsed. Of course we started the Faire to call attention to our program in the classics and to raise a little money for the department. It seems to grow every year with the participation of the other departments of the college and everyone seems to enjoy doing it. The Music Department loves to showcase their talent and of course the Drama Department has a chance to perform. It just seems to fall together. Everyone does their own thing about costumes with the help, of course, of the extensive collection in the Drama Department; and it's not as if lines must be learned since the speaking parts are read directly from a script of *The Prologue of The Canterbury Tales*."

"You have relieved my mind, Dr. Emily. Although I've always been a great fan of the theatre, I've never been an actor. Wouldn't want to let the department down and make a laughing stock of myself, you know." He smiled in a self-deprecating way that seemed contrived to Dr. Emily.

"Nonsense, you will do an excellent job. I assume you will be reading the part of Harry Bailey, Inn Keeper of the Tabard Inn. That's the part dear Dr. Stevens always played; and, naturally, as Chairman of the Department you will follow in his footsteps. Not that I want to pressure you, but it does give the whole thing continuity. I'm afraid people in the South put great store by things never changing too much."

"That's what I was afraid of, having to follow in his footsteps. At least my equestrian skills are topnotch if the acting is not what one would wish. Well, might as well make a good job of it, what?"

"That's the spirit," Dr. Emily responded. "I'll tell Glenda to prepare the sign-up sheet for the parts and have it posted in the hallway outside the department. You'll be amazed how quickly the parts will be snapped up. And by the way, I'll be sure and have Glenda fill in Elise's name for the Prioress. You will let her know, won't you?"

"You could always put her down as the Wife of Bath and say it was a mistake . . ." Basil's voice trailed off as a twinkle lit up his rather pale blue eyes. "Yes, the Wife of Bath; that would be rich!" His hearty laugh rang out in the room.

Strange, Dr. Emily thought, I think that's the first time I have ever heard him really laugh. Dr. Emily chuckled, "Oh that is naughty, but I'm afraid that part has already been filled. Glenda, bless her, insists that her womanly figure and her romantic conquests make her the only possible choice for the role of the merry widow. I think she will be perfect for the part and she seems excited about playing it."

Poor Basil, she thought, as she walked out of his office and toward her own cozy office at the rear of the building. Elise doesn't resemble the Prioress in the least, except perhaps her physical appearance. That's probably the reason she wanted to play the part of the character known for her beauty. The Prioress was a religious lady who had not given up the luxuries of the world and took great care in her physical appearance. No doubt Elise's vanity was involved, rather than her understanding of the character. The more she thought about Elise in the role of the Prioress, however, the more she realized that it might be a perfect match. Chaucer's understanding of human nature was as relevant in the modern world as it had been in his day. The Prioress and Elise Bowen might have had a great deal in common after all; neither was what she seemed to be.

And specially from every shire's end
Of England they to Canterbury wend,
The holy blessed martyr there to seek
Who helped them when they lay so ill and weak.
****

THE PROLOGUE OF THE CANTERBURY TALES
BY
GEOFFREY CHAUCER

Chapter 3

Jess Thornton, Merryvale College Chief of Police, sat in his patrol car just outside the college gates and reflected on the years he had spent trying to keep everyone on campus safe from the outside world. A good-looking man in his late thirties, he had returned to central Alabama after his military service and found a job on the campus police force. Within a few years, he was the Chief and had no desire to become upwardly mobile and move on to a big city police department.

For the most part he was content with his life. He had grown up in the country near Merryvale and the peace and quiet of a small Southern town suited him just fine; he had no desire to live anywhere else. True, he was still looking for the right woman to marry. In the meantime he had all the female companionship a man could desire, but somehow he had never met the woman he wanted to spend the rest of his life with. He had dated several of the ladies associated with the college; but those relationships, if you could call them relationships, had slowly died from lack of interest. On a few occasions he had been tempted by the younger women on campus; but he had never lost his head enough to ask one of them out, although they flirted with him outrageously.

Jess was too much of a professional to tempt fate by dating one of the students, although he noticed several of the more mature professors had robbed the cradle in the years he had been at Merryvale. If the truth were known, he supposed he had not been looking all that hard, content with the bachelor life; but lately he had his eye on Glenda McWilliams, the new secretary in the English Department. She was perhaps a few years older, but still a nice looking woman, he thought.

He eased his patrol car through the gates of the college and cruised across the old brick street toward Main Hall, the women's residence. One of the largest structures on campus and one of the oldest, it was an architectural gem, built when no expense was spared on materials and labor was cheap. It dominated the

Quad of the college and was the source of a multitude of stories of the lives of young women who had lived there, many no doubt based on truth, some on fantasy, but stories of triumph and tragedy none the less.

It was still early, but not too early for trouble, he thought. Jess had a sixth sense and was always on the lookout for anything that might disturb the peace of the campus. If anything out of the ordinary was brewing, he could almost smell it in the air. He continued to drive slowly around the old building, looking up at the dormer windows above the fourth floor; he slowed the car and finally stopped as he took a minute to gaze up at the rooms. Most of the time they were forgotten about; it had been years since any of the girls had lived up there. But no matter how long-ago it had been, there were still stories told about those two, long-vacant rooms, mostly legend and ghost stories.

The most common variation of the story was that in the early days of the college, when it had been an institution for women, a girl had burned to death or had committed suicide (no one seemed to remember which) in one of those rooms. Since that time no student had been able to live there for more than a day or two. Strange sounds were heard in the night; objects were moved by unseen hands; cold spots appeared in the rooms. It was really not unique in the lore of

Southern ghost stories; most campuses of any age had these tales.

The buildings on campus were old enough to have seen a great deal of life, Jess thought, and Merryvale took a great deal of pride in the fact that several of them predated the Civil War. Still, Jess was sensitive enough to understand how students would feel about living in those rooms, and he had to admit there was an unexplainable, otherworldly air about the campus, especially at certain times of the year.

A no-nonsense former military man and police officer, he had felt it himself as he climbed the stairs to the second floor of Rose Hall, one of the stately buildings that surrounded the Quad. It was said to be the oldest structure on campus, older even than Main Hall, and had been used as a Confederate hospital during the Civil War. On more than one occasion he had gone inside the antebellum building after hours to check out reports of suspicious activity, probably just students playing around, and had felt an unearthly presence.

It was an unnerving feeling, something he couldn't explain and had never spoken to anyone about—a feeling of unease, a movement caught in the corner of the eye, a coldness that gripped the heart. Simply imagination, he told himself, and was determined to believe that a trick of the mind was a reasonable explanation.

Jess was a down-to-earth kind of guy, but there were things he couldn't explain about Main Hall as well; one example was the lights that could be seen occasionally in the windows of those upstairs rooms. Even more mysterious was the coldness that was felt by everyone who had gone up the long flight of stairs to check it out, frequently on hot nights when summer school was in session. But most disturbing and hard to explain rationally was the sense of a presence in the rooms when an investigation was made. Wide-eyed students often reported seeing the lights, as did reliable adults and other campus police officers. They spoke in hushed tones as the story was told and retold. There was something about the campus, not just Main Hall, but the whole campus that at certain times of year took on an eerie atmosphere where time seemed to slip back and forth a little.

Jess shook his shoulders and muttered, "Nonsense," under his breath. It was a beautiful April morning. The grounds of the college were decked in the finery of spring. The air was heavy with the fragrance of thousands of blooming plants and shrubs as he made his rounds. Earlier he had watched as Dr. Goldman raced across the Quad to her eight o'clock class. Even

Dr. Goldman has spring fever, he thought, and gave a short chuckle under his breath. But it wouldn't be long before the campus would be turned upside down in preparation for the Canterbury Faire. Spring fever would not be an option then.

Like every year, Jess wasn't looking forward to the event, and worry about all that could go wrong had already begun to disturb his sleep. In other words he couldn't wait for it to be over. Create a mix of crazy college kids, absent-minded professors, visitors from far and wide, a large number of alumni (some suffering the infirmities of old age), along with a bunch of inexperienced riders on horseback—that was his take on the Canterbury Faire. It was a security nightmare; and it never ceased to amaze him that the administration approved of the whole event, even supporting the various spin-off celebrations after the reenactment of the pilgrimage, some of which in the past had gotten a little bit out of hand.

Last year some of the participants had started celebrating the night before, and Jess had still tipsy pilgrims on horseback the next morning to add to his problems. It was indeed a miracle that there had never been the slightest injury except for the pains of overindulgence. He hoped this year would be the same and that the pilgrims would all be in one piece when the day was finally over to give thanks for another year of successful fundraising and frolic.

Jess pulled his patrol car into an empty parking place in front of Tutwiler Hall and headed up the stairs to the English Department.

"Mornin', Glenda." Jess eased himself into the armchair next to her desk. He looked at her and gave her a quick wink. "How's the Wife of Bath this morning?"

Glenda gave him a sultry smile. "Better than ever," she purred.

"Do you know if Dr. Bowen has worked out a security plan for the Faire? I'm assuming we'll follow the plan already in place from past years, but thought I better drop in and discuss it with him. Don't want to go over his head and talk to Dr. Emily about it. Of course, Dr. Emily will have the final word. She always does." Jess smiled at Glenda.

"It does seem like she knows what she's doing. In the short time I've been here, since Dr. Bowen became department head, I've noticed how she seems to have the answers to all the questions that come up during the day. Actually, I'm surprised she's not the one in charge. She would be a great boss to work for."

"Didn't you know? The Board of Trustees offered her the position. She turned them down flat. She wouldn't touch that with a ten-foot pole. Dr. Emily is too smart to take on any job as an administrator. Some members of the Board wondered if she was up to the job, but let me tell you something; she runs this department anyway. She may seem like an academic with her head in the clouds, but she knows a good bit about life, and she knows how to handle herself." Jess leaned slightly toward Glenda's desk. "Dr. Emily is great. How about lunch?"

"I can hardly wait," Glenda said with a sultry smile.

"Good! If Dr. Bowen is busy I can come back this afternoon. This is really just a courtesy call."

"Why don't you do that, after our lunch date? He's with his wife right now. We probably shouldn't disturb them. They seem a little out of sorts if you ask me. I walked by his door a little while ago and it sounded like the fur was about to fly!" Glenda grinned at Jess and waved her hand back and forth to indicate it was a hot topic.

"Everyone seems to be having their problems this morning. I saw Dr. Emily rushing across campus to her eight o'clock class. Do you suppose she was actually late?"

"She made it on time, I think," Glenda chuckled. "I saw her flying down the hall to her classroom a few minutes ago."

"Back to our lunch date, can you meet me at The Mill on Main Street around noon? I'll be on call, of course, but hopefully everything will be quiet and we can enjoy their good food."

The phone on Glenda's desk gave two short rings. As she reached for the receiver, she gave Jess a look and waved her fingers at him. "See you then."

Full well she sang the services divine,
Intoning through her nose, becomingly;
And fair she spoke her French, and fluently,
After the school of Stratford-at-the-Bow,
For French of Paris was not hers to know.
****

THE PRIORESS
THE PROLOGUE TO THE CANTERBURY TALES
BY
GEOFFREY CHAUCER

Chapter 4

Really, Elise thought, as she walked out of Basil's office with only a cursory nod to Glenda. Always sucking up to that old maid, Dr. Goldman. Why should he, the department head, have to ask her permission for me to play the part of the Prioress? He's weak she thought; hopeless really, but at least he's biddable. He'll do as I say without realizing I'm the one who's calling all the shots. I wonder how long I can put up with being in this godforsaken place. Alabama, of all places! It's the back of beyond. Certainly not what I expected when I married an Oxford man, but surely I can figure out some way to get him to agree to look around for another position. Her lovely forehead was creased with a frown, one that threatened to become a part of her permanent expression if she wasn't careful.

Elise had resisted the move to Alabama. In fact, she threw a fit. She thought Basil could have found a more prestigious school, and she was unhappy about leaving her home state. But since the rumors at the college in Virginia had persisted long after the unfortunate events had occurred in his department, he had insisted it would be best for everyone if he tried to make a new start somewhere else. That had been the one and only time she had not been able to influence him. The Dean probably told him he had to go. Struck a deal with him and promised to give him a good recommendation. Wasn't that the way it worked, just like in the corporate world? They all made sure their tails were covered. Every time she thought about it she felt her resentment grow.

Elise walked slowly down the steps of Tutwiler Hall. She felt slightly lightheaded from the sudden burst of anger she had felt about Basil and his weakness, or perhaps it was the medication she was taking for the depression that had enveloped her since they moved to Alabama. Opening the door to her BMW, the bribe she had demanded from Basil, she slid into the drivers' seat and headed the car toward home. The day stretched endlessly before her with no one to talk to or confide in.

At least I'll be the Prioress, the elegant pilgrim, she thought. To be cast in the role of anything but a beautiful and cultured woman would have been unacceptable to Elise. It was all important to her to have the starring role and to be dressed to perfection. And I'm an accomplished equestrian, she thought. I'll ride sidesaddle if they have one at the college stable, or if I have to I can rent one since there's still plenty of time. That would show them all and be much more authentic.

With nowhere else to go and a lonely day in front of her, Elise decided to change direction and head for the college stables. In her mind's eye she was daydreaming of the impression she would make dressed as the Prioress and riding sidesaddle and was anxious to make arrangements for a mount for the day of the Faire. Her need to feel superior to those around her was growing more pronounced, almost an obsession.

She had been to the stable a few times to ride with Basil and had tried to present herself as an accomplished horsewoman, although in reality she had little riding experience. Although she tried to conceal it, she was afraid of horses, and they seemed to pick up on her fear, becoming nervy and restless around her. It didn't help that her insecurity gave her the feeling that the man in charge of the stable had taken an instant dislike to her. So typical, she thought; the people on this campus are so insular and suspicious of outsiders. Poor Elise had yet to understand that she was the one with the attitude that set everyone on edge and made them pull away from her.

The college stable, located on the western edge of the campus near the college lake, had a long history. During Merryvale's early years as a girls' school, the stable had housed the horses that the more affluent young ladies brought with them to the college, and many happy memories were made there. The land surrounding the college lake was crisscrossed with trails and was a lovely place to ride. Students, college faculty, and staff, along with a few local residents boarded their horses, making the college stable a popular part of campus life. Instead of being a drain on the college budget, the stable made a small profit each year and was the primary source for the equine participants in the Faire. Additional horses would be borrowed from local people if more were needed.

As Elise drove toward the stable, she made plans for her role as the Prioress. She would look over the horses that would be available for those who were not owners of their own mount, she thought. She also wanted to talk to Rich Henry, the caretaker at the stable, about a sidesaddle and a gentle but spirited animal. It must be an attractive horse, one to match the looks of the Prioress; and she needed to start thinking about her costume, she thought. Surely they had something she could use in the wardrobe of the drama department, but if not, she could always make a trip to Birmingham or to Montgomery if she couldn't find something suitable. With the Shakespeare Theatre located only an hour's drive away, surely there would be a decent costume rental in the area.

After all, she had to think about her position. As the department head's wife she felt a vague sense of obligation to help Basil, but vanity was the real driving force behind most of Elise's actions. She took great pains to remind everyone of her important social position back in Spotsylvania County, implying that no matter how hard they tried in this little backwater place they would never be able to do anything as well as the aristocratic class of her native state of Virginia. This didn't exactly endear her to people of Merryvale.

As she drove toward the college stable she began to brood about how she had gotten herself stuck in what she considered the middle of nowhere. When she married Basil, he had seemed quite a catch, a professor at a prestigious college in her home state and, more impressive, an Oxford man. Now she supposed she would have to face the fact that he was one of her biggest disappointments. She had never really loved him, and now she admitted to herself that she had made a serious mistake in marrying him. Like many of the other women who had pursued him on the campus in Virginia, she had been taken in by his good looks and that upper class British accent. I'll simply have to make the best of it for a little longer, she thought.

Elise had believed when she married Basil that he was the man she had been searching for, the man to provide her with a distinguished position in society. Of course, Basil was not a wealthy man by any stretch of the imagination. College professors were notoriously underpaid compared to other careers, but there was a certain prestige in being married to a graduate of the famed Oxford University in England and a respected member of the academic community in Virginia.

Unfortunately things had not worked out as she had planned, and now in his new position at Merryvale College she was frustrated and embarrassed that he wasn't taking charge in the department, even allowing himself to be told what to do by an elderly faculty member. She would be sure to talk to him when he got home that evening about asserting some authority and not letting Dr. Goldman get all the credit for the Faire.

As she pulled up to the paddock gate, Rich Henry walked slowly toward her car, a scowl of displeasure on his face. He had met her a few times when she and Dr. Bowen had come to the stables to ride. Rich was an unpretentious man, an animal lover, more at home with horses than with people, but a man who had an innate understanding of human nature. He could spot insincerity a mile away. He wasn't sure about Dr. Bowen yet, but he knew without a doubt that Elise Bowen was a phony. In addition to her insincerity his instincts told him that she was one of those women who could be dangerous if crossed, and he wanted to avoid contact with her as much as possible.

Rich had summed both of them up on the first day they came to the stable. Dr. Bowen knew what he was doing around horses, and the animals could sense his confidence. Rich could tell that right away and, as a result, thought that the man could be trusted around the animals and would treat them well. His wife, on the other hand, was nervous around them; and, of course, the animals picked up on that, becoming restive and skittish. He knew immediately that she had little if any experience with horses, although she tried to pretend to be a good rider. Watching her approach, he slowly walked toward the gate of the paddock. Trouble's on its way, he thought.

"Good mornin', Mrs. Bowen. What can I do for you?" His demeanor was polite but not exactly welcoming.

"Well, the first thing you can do is open the gate. I want to look at the horses. I'll need to borrow one for the Faire."

Elise looked him over in a way that would have made some people uncomfortable. It didn't faze Rich. He had lived in the white man's world long enough to know how to play the game. The South had changed a great deal since the days of his youth, and he was grateful that it had; but he was still wary of becoming too familiar with people, especially outsiders. If Rich didn't know a family, white or black, he took his time before warming up to them. He shifted his weight from one foot to the other, reached for the gate, and then withdrew his hand as if he had just thought of something. Better to get rid of her as soon as possible, he thought.

"Won't be any use looking at the horses. You're not allowed to just pick one out without permission. Most have been reserved for the Faire for months. You'll have to put your name down on the list in Dr. Bowen's office requesting a horse for the day. Then horses will be assigned from the stable once we have the list. If we need more animals we have several local people who are willing to help us out. Dr. Goldman always handled that part of it. I don't have any say about which horse folks ride."

Elise seethed. Dr. Goldman again! She couldn't seem to get away from the woman. "It does seem that someone could have told Dr. Bowen. I'll speak to my husband about the list and the fact that no one has informed us about proper stable procedure." She gave him a look that insinuated that he was somehow at fault. "What about an extra sidesaddle? I guess it's too much to ask if we have one available."

"Well, you can ask, Ma'am, but I don't recommend riding any of our animals with a sidesaddle. It takes an experienced rider to handle a horse sitting sideways. Besides, none of ours are used to it. It feels different to them, you know. Kind of throws off their center of gravity. Now a horse that's used to the sidesaddle— that's a different matter, but none of our horses have ever been saddled with one. I sure don't recommend it; and, besides, like I said, you need to be an experienced rider."

"I asked you a question! Do we have a sidesaddle in the stables, or will I have to borrow or rent one? And for your information, I am an experienced rider!" Elise's voice was shrill and her face was flushed with anger.

"Well, we do have one somewhere. It hasn't been used in a long time. It would have to be checked out. But I don't think you should try it. As I said, a lady needs to be an experienced rider. I wouldn't agree to saddle one of our horses for you, Mrs. Bowen, if you are determined to try to ride sidesaddle. Wouldn't want to be responsible." Rich kept his voice low, totally in control; but inside he was growing angrier by the minute. He hated the way she talked down to him.

Without a word Elsie turned and marched back to her car, slid under the wheel, slammed it into reverse, and floored it. The back wheels of the BMW spun as she cut the steering wheel and backed onto the grass at the edge of the drive, cutting ruts in the moist earth before she turned and sped down the drive toward the main road.

"Bitch!" muttered Rich under his breath. "There goes hell on wheels!"

But none the less, whilst I have time and space
Before yet farther in this tale I pace,
It seems to me accordant with reason
To inform you of the state of everyone
Of all of these, as it appeared to me,
And who they were, and what was their degree.
****
THE PROLOGUE OF THE CANTERBURY TALES
BY
GEOFFREY CHAUCER

Chapter 5

Dr. Goldman loved the privacy of her office and the sanctuary it provided during her day at the college. Her little Victorian house, only two blocks from campus, was her refuge away from her busy days; but her office, like her home, was a reflection of her taste. She had taken great care in furnishing it with the things she treasured: family antiques, photographs, original art. It was an eclectic mix and no doubt would have met with the approval of a professional decorator, although that had not been Dr. Emily's intention.

Order and aesthetics had always been her priority and was part of who she was professionally, but her day had certainly not begun as she had planned. The rush to get to her eight o'clock class had started her off on the wrong foot. She couldn't remember the last time she had overslept and vowed not to let it happen again.

Thankfully, her schedule for the day was fairly light. She had a class at eleven and would keep her office hours as usual. Checking her day planner for the afternoon, she was pleased to see she had no appointments scheduled, although there was always the possibility of a student or two dropping in to seek her advice on a paper or on their research.

With at least an hour before her next class and most of the afternoon to mull over plans for the Faire, she could relax and catch her breath. She would have to check with Glenda to be sure a sign-up sheet had been posted in a prominent place, she thought; but that was the only thing pressing at the moment. This gave her time to sit and reflect on the events of the past few days.

Turning slowly in her desk chair, Dr. Emily looked through the large window that graced her office. She was so thankful the twelve-foot ceilings had not been lowered in Tutwiler Hall and the building had not been modernized. As a result, the architectural features were a feast for the eyes. The window, in the Palladian style, looked out over the green lawn of the Quad toward the new library. The massive old trees with their fresh spring leaves were soothing to the eye. Just like an Impressionist painting, she thought, as she spun her chair back around to her desk.

She let her eyes roam around the office. The original wide board floors, polished to a deep glowing patina, were partly covered with one of her favorite oriental rugs. Its ruby-toned, intricate design gave warmth and a focal point to the room. The walls were lined with a small part of her huge collection of books. A few original oil paintings were artfully arranged between two of the bookcases, along with her diploma from The University of Chicago and a few family mementoes.

"My sanctuary," she sighed.

Dr. Emily's office may have been a place of peace and reflection; but on this morning in early April, worry about the department and the details of the upcoming Faire were disturbing her usual calm, contemplative mood.

She turned back toward the window just in time to observe Judson Sharp crossing the Quad toward the library. Something's not right with Jud. The thought, one that had occurred to her on several occasions during the last few months, especially at the end of the fall semester, struck her as being one more thing that she needed to check into before the end of the day.

What had begun as a vague concern about a promising student who seemed to have lost his way suddenly became of vital importance. She watched him through her window as he slowly mounted the steps to the school library. How many students had she worried about over the years? No matter, that was part of the responsibility of an educator, she thought, to encourage and support each student and treat them with compassion. She couldn't understand instructors who remained cold and aloof, never taking an interest in the personalities of their students, their hopes, their dreams.

Jud Sharp had come to Merryvale College as a transfer student at the end of his sophomore year and had continued his exemplary academic career. Now in his senior year, Dr. Emily had great hopes for his work on the graduate level and was looking forward to helping him in any way she could. She had written a letter of recommendation to several graduate programs, one of which was to her alma mater; and she could barely contain her pleasure that he was planning on a study of Anglo Saxon and Middle English literature. To say that she had great hopes for him was an understatement. He was her protégé, she supposed. He, in his modest way, was grateful that someone he admired so much had taken an interest in him.

Something is troubling Jud, Dr. Emily thought as she leaned forward in her chair to follow his progress across the campus. Not that his work was suffering, far from it. If anything he seemed to have immersed himself even further in his studies, rarely joining in the social events that revolved around the English Department. She had also noticed that recently he seemed to have developed a reticence about lingering in the office and passing the time of day. This was an obvious departure from the norm since he had been one of the most outgoing student assistants any one could remember, with a quick wit and a sunny disposition. Now, all was changed. It had done no good to ask if something was troubling him. She had tried on several occasions to get him to open up to her, but he had brushed her off with a, "Don't worry; I'm fine," response. After observing his dejected figure going up the library steps, she resolved to find out what was troubling him.

Dr. Emily tilted her chair back at a more comfortable angle and continued to gaze across the campus. What a tranquil place, she thought, but how deceiving that sense of tranquility could be. It seemed to her that the harmony of the English Department had somehow been lost. She hated to think that this had been caused by the change in the department head, but there seemed to be no other explanation. Most transitions are difficult, she realized, especially when there had been no changes in staff in such a long time. Still, two new faces in the department: Dr. Bowen and Glenda, the replacement for Mary Alice Lindstrom, who had retired last year when Dr. Stevens announced his retirement, had brought with them a change in the whole atmosphere of the department. Change is never easy, something we all resist, she thought.

Dr. Emily closed her eyes and thought about the unfortunate events that had taken place just in the academic year to date. Outward appearances may have seemed tranquil, but the year had not gotten off to a great start. Dr. Bowen had taken up the reins of the department and ruffled feathers within a few weeks of his arrival. Without consulting with anyone and with only a few days left before the beginning of the fall term, he made changes in teaching responsibilities; and many of these had been met with resistance and hurt feelings. He had let it be known from the beginning that he thought a department grew stagnant if certain professors taught the same courses year after year.

Dr. Aquilla Greer, second only in seniority to Dr. Emily, had fought to no avail to keep his long-held classes on the Romantic Poets and Victorian Literature. His reassignment to lower-level courses had not been taken well, to say the least; and Dr. Emily was worried that he would take an early retirement. Dr. Greer was a widely published, highly regarded expert on the Victorian Period, and this came as a great insult to him. To say he was angry and that there was an undercurrent of hostility was not an overstatement.

And then there was Dr. Melanie Adams, assistant professor of American Literature, a soft spoken, pleasant young woman, who had been highly offended when Dr. Bowen said that he thought American Literature was not worth very much. Actually, in no uncertain terms he let it be known that he looked down on Dr. Adams's favored works by William Faulkner and Eudora Welty and had made several comments about the superiority of the British writers to the Americans. It was unfortunate that these remarks had been made in front of a significant number of faculty and students at one of the open houses held by the English Department. With his Oxford accent and his aloof manner in public, Dr. Bowen had not endeared himself to his new colleagues, and for Dr. Adams it was an insult that perhaps could never be forgiven.

Dr. Emily longed for the laissez-faire days of former department head, dear Dr. Stevens. Ah, but that is a typical sign of old age, wishing for a return to the past and not looking forward to the future, she mused.

Perhaps Dr. Bowen had a point about teaching becoming stale if the same professors taught the same subjects year in and year out, in which case, the decision for change could be justified. But it was tactless and hurtful not to wait until his first year as department head was over before reassigning Dr. Greer. As a result, more than a few people questioned his administrative skills and his ability to work well with his colleagues.

As for the other, the insult to American Literature, Dr. Emily was afraid that would never be overcome, a terrible faux pas. She wished Dr. Bowen had used better judgment. Not for the first time she thought that there was arrogance about the man that was highly unattractive and would be offensive to most people. On the other hand, with his handsome features and polished air, Basil Bowen could be quite charming when he desired.

The quiet of her office and the pleasant hum of bees outside her window made her feel drowsy, and she caught herself as she almost dozed off. Really, I must quit this senseless worry, she told herself. Dr. Bowen's decisions and the problems they have created are out of my control. She collected her briefcase, locked her office door, and set out for her last class of the day. Surely, I will get some sleep tonight.

As she stopped in the hall outside the English Department office, she noticed that Glenda had posted a sign-up sheet for the Faire. She was gratified to see that many of the more interesting parts had already been snapped up by eager participants. No need to worry too much about Glenda fitting in and knowing exactly what needed to be done. We're fortunate to have found her. She seems to have everything in the office well in hand, Dr. Emily thought, as she entered her classroom and greeted her 11 o'clock class.

For he would rather have at his bed's head,
Some twenty books, all bound in black and red,
Of Aristotle and his philosophy
Than rich robes, fiddle, or gay psaltery.
****

THE CLERK
THE PROLOGUE OF THE CANTERBURY TALES
BY
GEOFFREY CHAUCER

Chapter 6

The wail of a distant siren cut through the late afternoon as Dr. Emily walked across the Quad toward the main gate of the college. She had kept her office hours in the afternoon and was now looking forward to a quiet evening and an early bedtime, but the events that were about to unfold would haunt her thoughts for days to come. It would be a long time before she would rest easily and sleep through the night.

Her first impression was that there must have been an accident involving one of the workers at Harmon Hall, the boy's dorm located just within the main gates. The building was not as old as some of the others on campus and had more modern amenities; but there had been a series of problems since its construction, and now it was undergoing a complete renovation. Two campus police cars and a small group of people had gathered in front of the dorm. Voices were low and there was a sense of gravity as Dr. Emily approached the group.

"What's happened? I hope no one is hurt," Dr. Emily addressed the group.

"No one knows for sure, Dr. Goldman," one of the students replied. "We were in our art class, sitting on the grass over there," she said, pointing to a spot in the middle of the Quad, "drawing the facade of Main Hall when two police cars pulled up." The wail of the siren drew steadily closer and was suddenly silent as paramedics arrived, jumped out of the vehicle, and raced up the steps of the building. Close behind was the truck from the City of Merryvale Fire Department.

"Chief Thornton was the first to arrive. We saw him run up the steps. It couldn't have been more than five minutes ago, but it seems like longer," another one of the art students said.

"Jess Thornton will know what to do if there has been an injury to one of the workers. He was a medic during his time in the military," Dr. Emily said, sensing the need for reassurance that they all felt.

With a population of around five thousand including students, faculty, and staff on campus, it was not unheard of for an ambulance to be called for various emergencies throughout the school year. Dr. Emily remembered that one of the professors in the music department had a minor heart attack during the fall semester, and a student had broken a leg while sliding down the bannister in Main Hall. On both occasions the wail of an ambulance has signaled that something was amiss.

Typical of a small town where nothing much ever happens, the group gathered outside the dormitory waited; and as time passed, their number increased. None of the onlookers could say afterwards that there was a sense of foreboding in the group, but at the same time none seemed to be able to turn away and go about their business. Everyone wanted to know what had happened and what the outcome would be. More students and a few more faculty members joined the growing crowd curious to see what was going to happen next.

"Wonder what's taking them so long?" one of the young men standing near Dr. Emily asked.

"It must not be too serious," she replied, "or they would be rushing out to get the person to the hospital."

A small number of students grew bored and drifted away. The consensus was that one of the workmen must have suffered a minor injury.

"Here comes Chief Thornton," the young man at Dr. Emily's side said in a voice that carried over the group and attracted Jess Thornton's attention.

"Keep back everyone. We're bringing someone out."

"Just as I thought," said Dr. Emily, "one of the workmen. I hope he's not injured too badly, poor man." Her gentle face registered her sincerity.

The paramedics wheeled a stretcher through the doors of the dorm, placed the patient in their vehicle, and drove through the college gates, picking up speed and turning on the siren as they went. The small crowd began to disperse. A few futile attempts were made to try to find out the identity of the patient and what had happened; but when it became clear that Chief Thornton was not giving out any information, the group drifted away.

Jess took Dr. Emily's arm and walked with her until they reached a bench under one of the old oaks that graced the Quad. "I'm afraid this will come as a shock, Dr. Emily."

Jess looked at her sweet expression, her flushed round cheeks, and the blue eyes slightly moist with compassion. Her concern was written on her face. The curls of her closely cut, white hair stood out around the edges of her beret like a halo. But he wasn't fooled. Jess knew all about Dr. Emily. He knew she was not as innocent as she looked and that she had a will of iron. Over the years he had confided in her on numerous occasions, and she had never betrayed his trust. She had helped him handle several delicate cases when students had run afoul of the law, and he respected her sense of fairness. They shared the philosophy that a student's life should not be ruined by one stupid act or indiscretion, and together they had built a partnership of sorts. It was not an official partnership, of course, but one that they both valued. Today, it would be put to the test again.

"It's Jud Sharp," he said.

Dr. Emily drew in her breath and put her hand on her breast. She felt her heart race momentarily and then tears began to well up in her eyes. "I knew something was wrong. What happened, Jess?"

Somehow she sensed the worst and that what had happened today was connected in some way to Jud's change in personality and his withdrawal, but she was having trouble controlling her emotions and already was beginning to blame herself for not doing something about Jud's depression.

"It was a suicide attempt, Dr. Emily. No doubt about it. He left a note." Jess reached over and took her hand in his. He was worried about the shock this might cause her. Dr. Emily was not a young woman, and he knew that her tender heart had been broken too many times. Her students are her life, he thought. They're like the children she never had, and he was aware that she had great hopes for Jud Sharp. He was someone to follow in her footsteps in the academic world, a continuation of her legacy, he realized.

"Several of the young men on his hall found him in his room unconscious. You know he has one of the private rooms reserved for senior men. Earlier in the afternoon he told one of the boys he was going to sleep and get up later to study. That he didn't want to be disturbed. I'm assuming that there must have been some concern about him on the hall since after a few hours one of the boys was elected to check on him. When they couldn't get a response from him, the pass key was collected from the resident assistant and his door was unlocked. They found him on his bed—an empty bottle of prescription sleeping tablets on the night stand. A handwritten note was on the bed next to him. All indications are that it was an attempt to take his life. There doesn't seem to be any indication of foul play. Of course it is very early in the investigation."

The normal color was beginning to come back into Dr. Emily's cheeks; and although a few tears had rolled down her face, she had bravely mopped them away with a handkerchief. Jess thought Dr. Emily was probably one of the last women in the world to still carry a real cloth handkerchief in her bag. She took a deep, shaky breath and sat up straight on the bench. Then she gave her shoulders a little shake, reminding Jess of a small terrier on the lookout for something interesting to chase.

"What did the note say, Jess?"

"Apologies for hurting the people that care about him, can't go on living, that kind of thing. It was the usual sort of note. No real reason given."

"And you think you got to him in time? You think he will recover?"

"Yes, I think he'll be all right. His breathing was very shallow when I got to him. I couldn't rouse him, so I called for backup. The paramedics got here pretty quick. They say he'll be okay once they get him to the hospital and get the meds out of his system. I don't suppose you know what was going on with him?

"I feel so bad about this, Jess. I knew there was something wrong and tried to get him to open up and talk to me about what was troubling him. There's been such a change in his personality. When he first came to us his junior year, he was a great favorite, very outgoing. But since before the Christmas break, he had become so withdrawn, not himself at all. I couldn't reach him; and now if he doesn't recover, I will never forgive myself. I should have done something!" Another tear rolled down Dr. Emily's cheek and a sob shook her short, rounded frame. For just a moment she looked like an old woman as a shadow of grief crossed her face.

Jess squeezed her hand gently and put an arm around her shoulders. "Don't feel like that, Dr. Emily. You did all you could. You tried to help. Sometimes things are beyond our control; there's nothing we can do about them. I learned that when I was in the Army. You see so much happen, and you wish you could change it. It doesn't usually work that way, you know. Don't blame yourself."

"You're always so comforting, Jess," she sighed. "I think I need to go home and lie down for a bit."

"Come on, I'll drive you home," he said as he took her arm, helped her up from the bench, and escorted her to the car. "You don't need to walk home by yourself."

"Thank you, Jess. On this one occasion I will let you pamper me. I must say, I never thought I would have to be driven home in a police car!"

Jess helped her into the front seat and drove slowly through the gates of the college and down Middle Street to her house. The house looks just like her he thought for probably the hundredth time. Something from the past that is precious. He parked in front of the cheerful yellow Victorian with the gingerbread trim and came around to help her out of the car and up the sidewalk.

"I'm all right now, Jess. You don't have to treat me like an invalid."

"Just let me see you inside and make us both a cup of tea before I go," he said. "I know you're strong, but you've had a shock. Then I want you to lie down and rest for a while."

"I won't argue with you. But something is still not right about all of this. The whole thing doesn't make any sense to me."

"It never does," Jess replied.

"No, no, about the note Jud wrote. What is it? There's something important I must remember about that. I just can't think clearly right now."

Jess took Dr. Emily's keys out of her hand and unlocked the front door. Max rushed into the room, anxious to play his part as protector of the house. He looked at Jess suspiciously and gave a sharp bark.

"It's only me, Max," Jess reassured the dog. "Your mistress needs some attention. Just give her a minute to sit here on the sofa." Max immediately jumped up next to her and snuggled as close to Dr. Emily as he could get.

Once they were seated on the sofa in her small sitting room, Jess went into the kitchen and started preparing the tea, making sure both cups had two teaspoons of sugar. Hot sweet tea was one of the best restorative drinks for shock, Jess believed. At least that was what his grandmother had always told him, and he was sure Dr. Emily was from the generation that shared those tried and true methods.

When the water boiled he poured it over the tea bags and sugar and placed each cup on a small silver tray he found on the kitchen table. There was probably a proper tea pot somewhere in Dr. Emily's kitchen, but Jess had not taken the time to find one, thinking she needed the drink as soon as possible. He wondered if she had any brandy in the house, but would wait and see if the hot tea did the trick. He worried that she still looked pale and drawn.

After giving the tea bags a few dips up and down in each cup, he discarded them and carried the tray into the sitting room, placing it on the low table in front of the Victorian sofa where Dr. Emily sat with the devoted Max. He could almost see the wheels turning in her lively mind and immediately felt better about her, although he still watched her carefully.

"Drink this, Dr. Emily. It's not brewed in a pot, but it's hot and sweet."

"Thank you, Jess." She raised the cup to her lips.

"Careful. It's hot!" Jess cautioned. "Don't worry, Max, your mistress will be fine." Max growled.

After several sips of the tea, the color returned to Dr. Emily's cheeks, and Jess noticed that her eyes seemed to have regained their old sparkle. For a while, Jess had been worried about the flat look of her eyes, a sure sign of shock, he thought. Now his patient seemed almost restored.

Not that Dr. Emily realized Jess was treating her as a patient and would have called for immediate medical attention if she had not shown signs of recovery. She simply viewed him as a kind man and a good friend, but he was also serious about his role as Chief of Police of Merryvale College, and from his perspective part of his job was the wellbeing of everyone related to the institution.

"I remember what was troubling me right after you told me that it was Jud and that he had attempted suicide," Dr. Emily said, placing her empty tea cup down on the table. "Why would he try to take his life if he was planning on playing one of the parts in the Faire? I looked at the sign-up sheet this morning and was so pleased that he had put his name down for the part of the Clerk. The only part for him, of course, since it describes him to perfection. Such a lover of books and learning and without a penny to his name. He's here on a full scholarship, you know. Have I told you I have great hopes for his academic career? He will probably receive a teaching assistantship to graduate school, perhaps at The University of Chicago, my old alma mater. We've been waiting anxiously to hear about his acceptance and possible financial aid. Why, I ask you, would he attempt to take his life with so much to look forward to? It doesn't make sense. There's something more to this whole thing. Something we don't understand." She reached over and rubbed Max's ears and scratched under his chin. The little dog's eyes closed contentedly.

"That's the kind of question most people ask when something like this happens, Dr. Emily. They think, they're so young, that they have so much to look forward to. I know it's hard to accept. But you mustn't upset yourself and take this so much to heart. Think of your other students. They need you, as well, you know. Are you feeling better, now? Is there anything I can do for you before I leave?"

Jess and Max studied her intently, both in their own way. It has been said that a Scottie is a one-person dog, and Max was no exception. He looked at Dr. Emily with the kind of devotion only a dog can give to his owner. He viewed Jess with undisguised suspicion, however.

"You've been so kind. I'm feeling much better, and your hot tea has certainly helped. I think I will read for a while and have an early night. Don't worry. Max will keep me company. I'm sure you have so much to do. Thank you for everything, Jess."

"Don't hesitate to call me if you need anything this evening," Jess said as he prepared to take his leave. "I'll see what I can find out about Jud's status; and if it's early enough, I'll stop by and let you know."

Later that evening Jess called to say Jud was still in the intensive care unit of the county hospital. His vital signs were almost normal, but he had yet to regain consciousness. His condition was guarded, but there was hope that he would make a full recovery.

Although the news was hopeful, Dr. Emily spent another restless night thinking about all the questions that must be asked in order to find out what had motivated Jud to attempt to take his life. First thing in the morning she would talk to Glenda about the sign-up sheet for the Faire. Perhaps Glenda had seen Jud when he wrote his name next to the part of the Clerk and could tell her something about how he seemed yesterday morning. Had she talked to him? Had he said anything out of the ordinary? Then she would meet with Dr. Bowen and see if he could shed any light on Jud's frame of mind. Jud had been in one of his classes the previous semester; perhaps he had noticed something. Finally, exhausted from the day, she drifted off into a fitful sleep with Max snoring on the foot of the bed.

A sergeant of the law, wary and wise,
Who'd often gone to Paul's walk to advise,
There was also, compact of excellence.
Discreet he was, and of great reverence;
At least he seemed so, his words were so wise.
****

THE LAWYER
THE PROLOGUE OF THE CANTERBURY TALES
BY
GEOFFREY CHAUCER

Chapter 7

Kevin Mitchell, County Sheriff and student of law, had heard the 911 call from the college on his police radio and instinctively turned his car toward Memorial Hospital. He immediately reached for his radio and called dispatch.

"On my way to County Memorial. Can you give me a location for Chief Thornton?"

"He's on the scene at the college, Sheriff Mitchell."

Kevin was patrolling the far eastern side of the county that afternoon. It had been a quiet day so far, but now he would have to meet Jess Thornton at the hospital and make a report before he could head for his night class in Montgomery. If something was going to happen in the county, it seemed it was always at the

66

end of his shift. He was in his last semester of law school and hoped to take the bar exam at the end of the summer. It wasn't easy working full time and going to law school at night, but he was about to reach the end of the goal he had set for himself and he could see the light at the end. This was just one more hurdle before the race was done.

Maybe Jess would make it to the hospital by the time he got there and they could file a report in time for him to make it to his night class. Although the campus police operated as a separate entity, the County Sheriff's Department still had oversight in any law enforcement matter that took place in its jurisdiction. Over the years, Jess and Kevin had become good friends and had worked closely on several cases.

"Sheriff Mitchell." His police radio crackled.

He picked up the receiver. "Mitchell," he responded. The radio crackled back to life.

"Chief Thornton will meet you at County Memorial as soon as he finishes up at the college and takes one of the faculty members who was at the scene back to her home. He says he will be there ASAP."

"10-4," Mitchell replied. Hurry up, Thornton, he thought.

Within a short time, he pulled into the emergency entrance of the hospital and parked the patrol car in one of the reserved spots. Let's get this over with, he thought. He extricated himself from the vehicle, shifting the twenty-pound belt that held his pistol, radio, handcuffs, and flashlight into a more comfortable position. He was a commanding presence in his uniform; and his six-foot, two-inch frame and lean physique caught the eye of everyone in the Emergency Room. One of the young administrative assistants fluttered over to him.

"Can I help you, officer?" she said with a bat of her eyes.

"Let me speak to the attending physician when he's finished treating the student they just brought in from the college. Let me know what his status is, if he made it or not, and let me know when Chief Thornton from the college arrives. He should be on his way by now. Page me when he gets here if I'm not around. My name's Mitchell, Sheriff Kevin Mitchell." He realized his manner was curt, but this was business, a young life was a stake, not a time to play around.

His serious manner put a halt to the young women's flirtatious look. This was a hospital, she remembered; and the patient they had just brought in was so young and vulnerable, close to her own age, she surmised. Confidentiality was hard to maintain in such a small hospital; the paramedics had called in requesting the

ER be prepared for an overdose, so she was aware that the patient had tried to kill himself. What could have been so bad that he would resort to suicide, she wondered?

"Of course, Sheriff. I'll personally see to it that you're kept informed." Her manner quickly changed from the flirtatious back to the professional.

Kevin thanked her, turned on his heel, and made a hasty retreat. He hated hospitals as much as he admired everyone who worked there. Just like his profession, hospital personnel must have a special calling to be able to do that kind of work day after day, he thought. At least I can get out in the fresh air; they have to deal with sickness and death in the confines of four walls. No wonder they can burn out so quickly.

He walked over to his patrol car and opened the glove compartment, took out a crumpled pack of cigarettes and lighter he kept there for just this sort of situation when the pressure of the job started to get to him. He didn't carry the cigarettes in his shirt pocket like most of the other officers who smoked. He tried to set an example, especially to the young people he came in contact with; but it was a hard habit to give up. He had gotten to the point where he was only smoking about five a day. Not too bad, he thought, but he was trying to give it up completely. Hard to do in his line of work. You either smoked or drank, or both, he thought in order to deal with the job. Not that the stress in their rural county could in any way compare with a big city like Birmingham or Atlanta. He took a couple of drags, impatient for Jess Thornton to show up. Finally, he saw the Merryvale patrol car turn into the entrance to the ER.

"What do you think happened?" he asked, barely giving Jess time to get out of his car. He ground the cigarette butt out on the pavement and, not seeing a receptacle, picked it up and put it in his pocket, disgusted with himself. "I thought you would've been right behind the ambulance."

"Obvious suicide attempt, Kevin. A promising kid in his senior year, English major, one of Dr. Goldman's favorite students. That's what took me so long. I wanted to make sure she got back to her house. She was in front of the dorm when they brought the boy out, and she took the news pretty hard. She seemed to be suffering from a mild case of shock. You know what a tender heart she has, and she's not getting any younger. Well, I couldn't leave her to walk home, could I? I wanted to make sure she didn't need anything. Gave her some hot, sweet tea and that seemed to restore her. She was pretty much back to normal when I left."

"Dr. Goldman has a big heart for such a small woman. I wish I'd been able to take more of her classes at the college, but I was focused on taking all of the political science courses I could squeeze in my schedule in hopes of getting into law school. So, there's no doubt in your mind that it was a suicide attempt?"

"No, he left a note. The empty bottle of sleeping pills was beside his bed. The other boys in the dorm said he had appeared to be depressed, that he'd not really been himself since back in the fall. Maybe we'll know more when we're able to talk to him. I take it he will recover?" Jess gave Kevin an inquiring look.

"We really don't know yet. I haven't spoken to the attending physician. Let's see if we can find him and get an update. Then hopefully we can get our paper work done."

"I thought you quit smoking?"

"Shut up, Thornton! It's just a little fall from grace."

*Now is it not of God a full fair grace
That such a vulgar man has wit to pace
The wisdom of a crowd of learned men?*
****

THE MANCIPLE
THE PROLOGUE OF THE CANTERBURY TALES
BY
GEOFFREY CHAUCER

Chapter 8

Dr. Emily was so preoccupied the following morning that she barely noticed the loveliness of the campus as she walked toward Tutwiler Hall. She was still shaken and sad about the disturbing events of the previous afternoon and was for once glad that the morning before her would not require her to lecture and answer questions. Fortunately, this was one of the mornings set aside each week for research. Like all professors in the academic world, she was expected to publish scholarly articles in her field of expertise in addition to the hours she was required to be in her office to assist students. When she wasn't lecturing or counseling students, she enjoyed the time spent on her personal research. Not surprisingly, she was writing an article for publication in an obscure journal devoted primarily to the study of Anglo Saxon and Middle English literature.

In the afternoon she would meet with her students doing independent study on a topic of their choice. Each student would delve into a literary period and produce a research paper that could possibly form the basis of more advanced study on the graduate level. Most students in this particular class would be working on advanced degrees in English after graduation with the goal of an academic career at the end of their studies.

The class met in her office since there were only three students enrolled this semester, a relaxed and cozy atmosphere. Normally, it was one of the high points of her week, one that Dr. Emily looked forward to with anticipation. Originally scheduled as a three-hour seminar, they often lingered much longer, so intense was the enthusiasm of the students for their respective research.

It was also a welcome chance for Dr. Emily to be able to visit with the senior-level students in an informal atmosphere, but it would be difficult to carry on with the class this afternoon since Jud was one of the members. The shock of Jud's suicide attempt and the empty chair at the seminar would, no doubt, affect them all.

She thought about cancelling the class as she walked carefully along the brick paving that led up to Tutwiler Hall, focusing on the walkway rather than on the riot of spring color. Her caution and attention to where she was putting her feet was not, however, a sign of advancing age. It was easy for a young person to take a spill on the uneven surface of the sidewalk. She was mindful of her steps, especially where the roots of the lovely old trees made the bricks rise up in waves. But this morning for the first time she began to feel the approach of the frailty of her advancing years.

Her normally ebullient spirit had received a blow, and the shock she had suffered when she found that Jud had attempted to take his own life was something that would mend more quickly when and if he was back in his place in her class. But at this point, Dr. Emily was not able to look that far into the future. She felt anxious and depressed.

Jud's absence from the class this afternoon would certainly cast a pall on the atmosphere, she thought; but for the sake of her other students she would have to put on a brave face and not allow their work to suffer, especially since the end of the term was growing near. With this resolve in place she planned to work during the morning hours on her article and then meet with the two remaining members of the seminar.

Finally arriving at Tutwiler Hall, Dr. Emily climbed the flight of stairs to the English Department with a heavy heart. She wasn't the only one suffering from melancholy it seemed. Glenda sat dejectedly at her desk in the office as Dr. Emily stopped to catch her breath and check her mail.

"I couldn't believe it," Glenda said as soon as she saw Dr. Emily in the doorway. "Jess Thornton called me at home last night and asked me some questions about Jud. Had I seen him recently? Did I think he seemed depressed? Of course, there really wasn't much I could tell him. I don't know Jud that well since I'm new here myself. I just can't believe it has happened again."

"It seems like a bad dream, doesn't it?" Dr. Emily responded. It took a few minutes for Glenda's words to sink in. "What do you mean, it has happened again?" she asked.

"What? Is that what I said?" Glenda frowned and moved a few things around on the top of her desk. "I was just thinking about something that happened back home. The same sort of thing except the boy died."

Dr. Emily took a closer look at Glenda. Normally, Glenda took a great deal of pride in her appearance. Dr. Emily thought that she usually looked like a pretty high- maintenance woman, one who spent a lot of time on her hair and makeup; but this morning she seemed to have let herself go a little. It was obvious she had been crying and her makeup was applied with less than expert care. A few smudges of mascara could be seen under her eyes, which only added to the dark circles Dr. Emily had never noticed before. Probably the result of a sleepless night, Dr. Emily thought. She must be taking this pretty hard.

"I suppose almost every community has experienced the loss of a young person in this way. Yes, it's very sad, Glenda. By the way, I was wondering, did you notice if Jud signed up for a part in the Faire yesterday morning?"

"As a matter of fact, I did. Funny you should ask. Jess asked me the same thing last night. I couldn't tell him very much about that either. I do remember Jud stopped by briefly and put his name on the list. From where I sit, I can't see the sign-up sheet out in the hall, but I just happened to be over by the window watering the plants and could see him stop and look at the list. I walked out into the hall to ask if he had decided which part to sign up for. It was just the normal sort of chit-chat. We didn't talk about anything important. I try to get to know the students and be friendly, show a little interest in them. I think that's part of my job in the department—to try to help them if I can. He said he had already made up his mind, that he had been planning it for months. He said he wanted to play the part of the Clerk since that character liked books more than anything else." Glenda became emotional again thinking about Jud and reached for a tissue to wipe at her eyes.

"Did he say anything else?"

"Let me think." Glenda sniffed and wiped at the last trace of moisture on her face. "As a matter of fact he did. He said he was excited about the Faire and couldn't wait to portray one of the pilgrims. That he'd been thinking about making his own costume."

"Yes, that's what I thought," Dr. Emily nodded.

"Oh!" Glenda exclaimed. She looked startled. "Now I see what you're getting at. Why would he leave here, after signing up for the part and talking to me about how much he was looking forward to it, and go back to his room and take an overdose? It doesn't make sense, does it Dr. Emily?"

Dr. Emily shook her head. "No, it doesn't Glenda. Not at all! I'll be in my office for the rest of the morning if anyone needs me." She paused in the doorway thinking that perhaps there was more to discover about Jud's actions on the previous morning. "Do you know if Jud left the building after he signed up for the part?"

She was thinking about seeing him yesterday morning from her office window as he walked up the steps to the library. That must have been somewhere between 9:30 and 10:30. She remembered rushing to her eight o'clock class and afterward going to her office and thinking over the events of the previous evening at Dr. Bowen's home. A short time later she had looked out of her office window, noticed Jud on his way across the Quad, and saw his dejected air as he went up the steps to the library. What on earth could have been going on in his mind, she wondered?

Glenda reached for another tissue and dabbed at her eyes. "No, I don't believe he left the building until after he talked to Dr. Bowen. I know he didn't have an appointment; at least he didn't go through me to make it. Let me think a minute, he signed his name to the sheet, told me goodbye, and walked down the hall toward Dr. Bowen's office. I saw him knock on the door and go in. It must have been around 10:15. That's the last I saw of him." The tears began to flow again.

"Forgive me, Dr. Goldman. Let me just step across the hall to the ladies' room and repair the damage."

"Of course, my dear. I'll stay here in the office in case anyone needs something until you return. Take your time."

What could have happened during Jud's interview that could have made such a change in his demeanor, Dr. Emily wondered. She must have seen him from her office window after he met with Dr. Bowen yesterday morning. Had something happened during that interview to upset the boy? Glenda thought he had been happy and enthusiastic before he had gone into Dr. Bowen's office.

On second thought perhaps it was just her imagination that Jud had seemed downcast. It was just an impression, after all, and she was seeing Jud from a distance across the Quad. Would it be possible to logically make an assessment about Jud's emotional stability simply by observing body language? She wasn't sure, but she wanted to find out what Basil Bowen knew about Jud's state of mind yesterday morning before she retreated to her office and prepared to work on her article.

Glenda returned to her desk looking pale but with the smudges removed from under her eyes and a fresh coat of lip gloss. Her eyes were a little swollen, and it was obvious she had shed a few tears, but she was back to looking more like her old self.

She'll be a perfect Wife of Bath, Dr. Emily thought. With the events of the last twenty-four hours on her mind, she had almost forgotten about the Faire.

"Is Dr. Bowen in this morning, Glenda?"

"Yes, I'm all but certain he's in his office. I saw him come in a few minutes after I got here. He didn't stop to talk like he usually does, but went straight down the hall. Unless he went down the back stairs, he's probably still there."

"Ring his office for me and ask if I may have a few words. I know he doesn't have an early class this morning, and we need to talk about a few things related to the Faire." Glenda doesn't need to know I want to talk to him about Jud, she thought. He may have been one of the last people to talk to him before he attempted to take his life. Perhaps he could shed some light on Jud's mood when he saw him. Anyway, it was worth taking a few minutes away from working on her article to see if she could discover some new information that might help Jess Thornton in his investigation.

"He says that will be fine. He can spare a few minutes, but that he does have a class to prepare for, Dr. Goldman," Glenda's voice brought her back to the present.

"Thank you, Glenda." Dr. Emily smiled warmly at her as she left and strode purposely down the hall to Dr. Bowen's office.

She wasn't really on friendly terms with the man, she thought, as she paused briefly at his office door. They had simply observed the social graces in a rather superficial way. And although she felt she had made an effort with him, his natural British reserve and aloofness had made it difficult to feel that they had begun to establish any sort of rapport. Obviously she wasn't the only one who felt this way since she didn't feel the camaraderie that existed in the department before he took over from Dr. Stevens. There had been all that unpleasantness about course assignments, and Dr. Bowen had unfortunately made those tactless remarks about certain people in the department and their taste in literature. All of this had created a tension, an undercurrent of dissatisfaction, that Dr. Emily hoped would soon be resolved.

Of course it was to be expected that with any change in the hierarchy of a department there would be a period of adjustment, and surely disagreements and slights would eventually be overlooked or forgiven after a good working relationship was established and a little time had passed. At least that had been her experience in the academic world that had been so much a part of her life for so many years. Now she thought there was the possibility that things had gone too far, that Dr. Bowen had so deeply offended several members of the department that the relationship was irreparable.

Dr. Emily decided she couldn't worry about the future relationship of the department head and faculty until the questions about Jud's suicide attempt had been answered. Until she had those answers, she was focused on finding out what had happened on the previous day when Jud visited with Dr. Bowen. Suddenly she felt empowered. This was something that needed to be discussed in the hope that somehow they could help Jud find his way back to them.

She knocked twice on Dr. Bowen's door.

"Come."

She heard his voice from behind the door, and she had second thoughts. She wondered if she should be asking him questions about Jud. Maybe it would be best to leave the investigation to Jess Thornton, but Dr. Emily was afraid that the whole episode would be written off as a failed suicide attempt and dropped after a few days had passed unless she pursued the matter. She felt instinctively that there was more to it, but she didn't know enough about what had been going on in Jud's life to accept that as an explanation. She was hoping that Dr. Bowen would be able to provide her with some answers to her questions. Taking a deep breath, she opened the door to his office and stepped resolutely across the threshold.

Dr. Bowen was seated at his desk with a haggard look about him. He's been affected by this tragedy as well, she thought. Perhaps I have misjudged him. It might be that British reserve that puts people off.

"Do sit down, Dr. Goldman. It's been a rather long night, I'm afraid. It's just terrible about what happened yesterday, such a shock to all of us. Of course, I barely know Jud. Can you believe Chief Thornton actually came by my home last night and disturbed our dinner to ask questions about the wretched boy? How am I supposed to know what's going on in a college student's head?" His hands moved restlessly across the papers on his desk.

Dr. Emily knew at this very moment that her instincts had been right. He's worried about more than Jud's suicide attempt, she thought; and with a flash of insight she realized that it was all about him. He is more distressed about how this has inconvenienced him, rather than with the welfare of one of our students. But she thought it might be more than having his dinner interrupted that was weighing on his mind and made him seem so tense and troubled. He's hiding something, something he is afraid will be revealed about the events of yesterday, she thought.

"Yes, I'm sure that must have been very trying for you, Dr. Bowen."

She decided to adopt a sympathetic tone, hoping he would take her into his confidence. "And I'm sure you must be worried about the impact this will have on the department."

"Well, of course, but the department had nothing to do with this, Dr. Goldman. What on earth do you mean?"

"It has been my experience that anything related to our students usually reflects on all of us, Dr. Bowen. The next question that will be asked is why we didn't know something was troubling, Jud. No doubt the Dean will be asking that of you before long. It's simply a matter of bad press, you know. It looks bad when our students are so unhappy they try to kill themselves. It affects our image, and we have a tendency to take that very seriously."

"You don't think many people know about this do you?"

"Perhaps not too many at the present, but that will change, Dr. Bowen. This is a small college, located in a small rural town. News travels fast and questions will surely be asked. Which leads me to the reason I stopped by this morning. I understand Jud had a meeting with you yesterday, and I wondered if you could shed some light on his state of mind when you saw him?"

"Well, yes, he did drop by for a talk." Dr. Bowen shifted uncomfortably in his desk chair, turning back and forth between looking out his window and facing Dr. Emily. "He was in my class last semester, The

History Plays of Shakespeare, you know. A good student—possibly a candidate for graduate school."

"I think he's much more than a candidate, Dr. Bowen. Jud will be offered several assistantships, I'm sure, and I fully expect him to continue his studies and complete his PhD, after he has finished his Master's Degree, of course. In fact, he's probably the most brilliant student I have ever taught. He has an ear for the Anglo-Saxon language and can already translate Middle English as well as many doctoral candidates in the field."

Dr. Bowen seemed annoyed with the course of the conversation, rose to his feet, and walked over to the window, turning his back on Dr. Emily as he spoke. "If you don't mind Dr. Goldman, I'm really too busy at the present to argue about the abilities of one of our students. I believe you wanted to know about the meeting I had with the boy." His back was still turned to Dr. Emily as he spoke. "He seemed perfectly normal to me. Certainly not depressed or in an emotional state. He came by to discuss one of our topics from last semester's class. That's all I know. Now if you will excuse me, I have matters that must be attended to and a class to teach in a few minutes."

"Of course, Dr. Bowen," Dr. Emily replied. "If you think of anything that might help get to the bottom of this unfortunate incident, I'm sure you will let me or Chief Thornton know."

Dr. Bowen turned from the window and stared at her. He could barely conceal his irritation. "I wasn't aware that you were working with the police, Dr. Goldman; nor was I aware that part of your duties at this college was to play detective." The sarcasm in his voice was poorly concealed.

"Let's just say I am an advisor to the police, both campus and county police to be exact. And as for my duty to the college, anything relating to our students, not just Jud, but any of our students, is part of my duty to this institution. Good day, Dr. Bowen." And with that said, Dr. Emily departed to the solitude of her office.

Meanwhile, as Dr. Emily was enjoying the time alone in her office, Dr. Aquilla Greer and Dr. Melanie Adams had by prearrangement met at the Coffee House in town and found a quiet corner to air their grievances against Dr. Bowen. Dr. Greer and Dr. Adams had suffered cutting criticism from the new department head, and this had drawn them together in a common cause. They both despised the man.

"We must be careful discussing this topic in public. I don't want to be overheard and create more trouble in the department," Dr. Adams said softly as they drank the freshly brewed coffee. She leaned across the table toward Dr. Greer and lowered her voice to a whisper. "From what I hear, the students are unhappy in his classes. A few have complained that there's not the depth of analysis of the literary selections that they expected and that they are intimidated when they ask questions."

"I'm hearing the same thing," Dr. Greer muttered. He glanced quickly around.

A group of students entered and nosily dropped books and bags on a table on the other side of the room.

"It's his arrogance that I find so offensive," Dr. Adams continued in a low voice. "I took his attack on American Literature as a personal insult, Dr. Greer! I can't remember when I've been so upset."

"Don't let them hear," Dr. Greer said as he made a gesture toward the group of students who were chatting happily among themselves.

"I don't believe they're paying any attention. Can you imagine how I feel? He thinks my area of expertise is worthless," she whispered.

"At least you're teaching your specialty! In essence, he has demoted me to lower-level courses." Dr. Greer's face became flushed. "My Victorian classes were turned over to a part-time instructor, for god's sake! His anger began to rise. "The man is an idiot!"

Dr. Adams became flustered. "Lower your voice, Dr. Greer," she pleaded.

"I don't care who knows my views. I hate the bastard! I wish he would drop dead!"

Heads turned at the student's table, and a few curious looks crossed the room.

"We should get back to campus," Dr. Adams said as they made a quick exit. "Let's talk later in a more private spot and discuss what we should do. We can't allow him to destroy the department, Dr. Greer. We need to get rid of the man! I suppose the first step would be to complain to the Dean.

Curious glances from the group of students followed the two professors as they hurried out the door of the coffee house. "I wonder what that was all about," one of them said.

She was at pains to counterfeit the look
Of courtliness, and stately manners took,
And would be held worthy of reverence.
****

THE PRIORESS
THE PROLOGUE TO THE CANTERBURY TALES
BY
GEOFFREY CHAUCER

Chapter 9

Dr. Basil Bowen paced the floor of his office after Dr. Emily left. His was a high-strung personality and now his nerves were shot. He was in over his head, and what made it worse was that he could blame no one but himself.

The previous evening had been one of the worst nights he could remember since his marriage to Elise. Jess Thornton's unannounced visit to his home asking questions about Jud's suicide attempt had done nothing but make him feel more trapped than ever. He wondered if the truth would come out now that the boy had survived.

He blamed Elise as he paced the floor of his office. She had driven him to this point by her excessive demands and her inflated perception of her social position, he fumed. It had not taken him long after the marriage to realize that she was somewhat of a joke back in her home state of Virginia. Always going on about her ancestors and their accomplishments and what a shame that she had to make do with being married to an academic? If only her family had not suffered such serious setbacks over the years, she told the unhappy people she managed to corner at social functions. Most people back at the college in Virginia had learned very quickly to avoid her at all costs, and as a result their social life had become almost non-existent.

Now the demands of the department at Merryvale were more than he had anticipated. Why had he listened to Elise and let her manipulate him, he wondered. Sometimes he felt that it would be much better if he just made a clean breast of everything. Admit to the world that things were not what they seemed.

That would be the end, of course: the end of his career, his marriage (not a great loss perhaps), his livelihood. He had mentioned it to Elise on a few occasions when she had almost driven him mad with her incessant lament about their lack of money. "I'm tired of the charade," he had told her. "What if I just pack it in and tell the truth?" He had thought it would all come to light after the trouble at the college in Virginia. But, miraculously, no one had discovered the deception. The truth, of course, was that it is extremely easy to fool people.

Last night had been one of the worst rows of their marriage. The argument had started soon after his arrival at the house.

"You're not being assertive enough, Basil. I went by the stables this morning and had words with that stable hand. Can you imagine? He actually had the effrontery to suggest that I'm not an expert rider!"

"Perhaps he's seen you ride," he responded with a sneer. "But what has that got to do with my not being assertive enough?"

"How dare you! You know I have been riding all my life. Daddy bought me a pony when I was only four years old. I really don't know what you would do without me, Basil. I had to learn from the stable hand that you're supposed to have a sign-up sheet in your office for the actors who'll need a horse on the day of the Faire. Because you've failed to do this, people who don't keep a horse at the stable or don't have one of their own have already reserved the most desirable horses, I suppose by getting it approved by the stable hand. What's his name?

"Rich Henry," Basil muttered.

"Whatever, in other words a man who works as a menial is making the decisions you should be making. I ask you, where does that leave me? Surely, you don't expect me to ride some broken-down nag?" Elise's lovely face was transformed as she spoke into the image of a petulant, dissatisfied woman.

"What difference does it make, Elise? It's only a college production, not a world premiere at Stratford-upon-Avon."

Like almost every other afternoon, this was just the beginning of the verbal assault directed toward Basil Bowen when he returned home from the college. When Jess Thornton arrived an hour or so later, the couple had called a momentary truce in order to sit down to dinner; but if past evenings were any indication, the hostilities would continue with after-dinner drinks.

"Who on earth can be calling at the dinner hour?" Elise complained as she rose from her seat at the table and stormed out of the room to answer the front door. Somewhat surprised to find the officer on her door step, she escorted Jess into the dining room.

"Officer Thornton is here, Basil," she said, giving her husband an inquiring look.

"I'm so sorry. I see I've arrived during your dinner," Jess said, feeling rather awkward since during the first few moments of strained silence that followed neither Basil nor Elise made an effort to make him welcome. "Perhaps I better come back a little later."

"That might be a good idea," Elise said.

"No, no," Basil replied wearily. "Could we offer you something to drink, officer?" Basil glanced briefly at his wife. "I'm sure Elise will be happy to get you some coffee or tea. Or perhaps you would prefer a sherry?" Elise looked at Basil with such contempt that Jess felt uncomfortable.

"No, thank you, Dr. Bowen. I'm making inquiries about your student, Jud Sharp. I'd like to ask some questions if you could give me a few minutes."

Basil looked startled as he pushed his chair away from the dining room table and rose to his feet. "Let's go into the parlor, shall we?"

His cool British reserve made Jess uncomfortable. He really does live in another world, Jess thought. Imagine, calling the room in their small house a parlor. Jess had always thought Dr. Bowen was too formal in his manner, but tonight he also seemed nervous and on edge.

"What about Jud Sharp?" Elise asked with a note of hesitation in her voice. "What about him...what's happened?" Jess noticed she had to steady herself by reaching out for one of the dining room chairs.

"He tried to kill himself," Jess said, carefully observing their reactions.

"Good god!" Basil exclaimed. The color seemed to drain from his face. "Please, Officer Thornton, let's retire to the other room."

With Basil leading the way, the three of them moved into the cramped room Basil called the parlor. It was comfortably furnished, but it had a temporary look about it, Jess noticed. Neither Basil nor Elise seemed to have spent much time adding any of the touches that make a house into a home. There were no family photographs or decorative items on display, no paintings on the walls. It had a sterile look about it. They must not be happy here, Jess thought. He sat down stiffly on the contemporary sofa without waiting for Basil or Elise to take a seat and pulled out the little notebook he kept in his shirt pocket. Basil had gone to the window and stood with his back turned to the room. Elise walked back and forth with what appeared to be pent-up energy or agitation.

"I have a few questions for you, and then you can get back to your dinner and your evening," Jess said, turning to a fresh page in his little notebook. At the top of the page he wrote: Basil Bowen. "Were you aware of any problems Jud Sharp may have been having, or did he perhaps confide in you, Dr. Bowen?"

Basil turned from the window and moved across the room to a chair opposite Jess. Glancing at Elise he threw himself down and let out a long sigh. "No, no, I can't say that I was aware of anything wrong with the boy. Of course, I don't know him very well. He was in one of my classes last semester. I must say I'm rather surprised by your visit tonight and that you're questioning people. It seems like every college campus has unfortunately had to deal with this kind of thing from time to time."

"That's true," Jess replied. "This is certainly not the first time we've had to deal with a troubled student who has attempted suicide, Dr. Bowen. But, fortunately, it doesn't happen very often on this campus. We like to think, and I know the faculty and staff would all agree with me, that we look out for our own."

"Well, yes. I'm sure that's the case, but what else can I tell you, officer? I certainly can't give you a reason for his actions. Who knows what's going on in a young person's mind?"

"I was hoping you could give me some insight into his behavior over the last few months. He's an assistant in the English Department, I understand; and I would imagine you see him on an almost daily basis. Have you noticed a change in his personality? Has his work suffered? Any information about him you could give me might help explain what's been going on with him and what made him want to take his own life."

"I'm sorry, Officer Thornton." Basil's face was pale and he looked shaken. "I can't think of anything that might be of help to you. He's just an ordinary student in the department. Actually, one I don't know very well."

"Not just an ordinary student, Dr. Bowen. According to Dr. Goldman, Jud is very gifted.

"Dr. Goldman perhaps has a tendency to think her students, especially the young men, are special, Officer Thornton. They probably appeal to her romantic nature, not really uncommon in elderly, sexually frustrated academics, I think."

"What Basil is trying to say is that she is a silly old maid," Elise sneered.

"Stay out of this Elise; that's not what I meant. I'm trying to explain to Officer Thornton that Dr. Goldman may not be highly objective about her students."

Jess didn't appreciate the way the conversation was heading and was offended at their mean-spirited, mocking attitude. "I appreciate your time, and I'm sorry I've disturbed your evening," Jess said, rising from the sofa and moving toward the door. "You may think you haven't been much help; but, in reality, you've given me several things to think about."

After biding them a curt goodbye, Jess took a few minutes to make a few notes of the comments made during their conversation before he started the car and headed home. He had been angered by their attitude toward Dr. Emily and detected an undercurrent of resentment in their attitude toward her that troubled him. What troubled him the most though was that not once had either of the Bowens inquired about the condition of Jud Sharp; not once had they asked how he was doing or expressed concern for his welfare. There's something not right about those two, he thought.

Yet for all he was philosopher,
He had but little gold within his coffer;
But all that he might borrow from a friend
On books and learning he would swiftly spend...
****
THE CLERK
THE PROOGUE TO THE CANTERBURY TALES
BY
GEOFFREY CHAUCER

Chapter 10

The doctors at County Memorial agreed that Jud Sharp had a very close call and by all rights was lucky to be alive. It had been touch and go for several hours after he had been brought to the ER, but he had a strong constitution and thanks to a rapid medical response eventually began to show signs of improvement. There had been some worry about complications since he was unconscious for so long, but his vital signs had been steady, and with time he slept it off and woke up in the ICU with a pounding headache.

After several days in the hospital, arrangements were made by the staff social worker, at Dr. Emily's suggestion, for Jud to spend a week or two in a residential rehabilitation facility where he could receive counseling after such an emotional trauma. There had been a great deal of discussion about what to do to help Jud during his stay at the hospital and an outpouring of compassion and concern from the college. Naturally, Dr. Emily readily stepped in to help make a few decisions in the absence of any close relatives. She thought about having him stay with her when he was released from the hospital, but on second thought felt that somehow that might not be the best idea. The rehab facility would undoubtedly give him the time and the professional support he needed, and she was assured it was a pleasant place where he could work on his college assignments when and if he felt able to continue his research.

Dr. Emily wasn't sure if she should bring up his academic progress during one of their early visits, but Jud had assured her that he wanted to get back to his studies in hopes he could make up for lost time and graduate on schedule at the end of May. As he had often said, his work was therapy; and he did some reading while he was in rehab. Not surprisingly, as soon as he was released, he threw himself back into his research. Dr. Emily, with a sigh of relief, was greatly encouraged by his determination to take up his work where he had left off and felt that the outlook was promising for his full recovery.

Her visits to him were frequent during his stay in rehab, and she enjoyed the time she spent with him, but she later reflected that she had learned no more about Jud on a personal level than she had known before his attempt at suicide. She did learn that he was basically alone in the world, but she still knew next to nothing about his family or their background.

What she did discover was that he was an emancipated minor by the time he was sixteen years old. One can only imagine the circumstances that must have led up to an emancipation decree at such a young age, she thought. That would have been during his high school days when so many young people from troubled families dropped out of school, but Jud beat the odds and somehow managed to graduate at the head of his class. He had lived with the family of one of his high school friends during his last two years of high school and, following his graduation, worked his way through junior college before coming to Merryvale.

So many terrible things could happen to young people, Dr. Emily thought. Perhaps for some the severing of family ties was for the best, especially if there had been some form of abuse involved; and she imagined that may have been the case with Jud, although this was sheer speculation on her part. She was a student of psychology and understood that some adults who had been abused as children had difficulty forming close relationships with others and standing up for themselves, believing that somehow the abuse was their own fault.

She thought this described Jud fairly well. He seemed to be afraid to let anyone get too close; and although he was liked by the other students, she was certain that he hadn't made any close friends since he had been at the college. Not that he could have been described as aloof or anti-social. He had a cheerful, pleasant manner before things started to go wrong during the past few months; but his mild manner and what seemed to be his need to seek approval through his work made it highly unlikely that he would ever have an assertive personality. He seemed to enjoy the interaction with students and faculty in the English Department, but Jud could best be described, if not as a loner, as a solitary figure, self-contained. Dr. Emily worried that he would find it difficult to cope with the hardships of life, but perhaps he would grow stronger and more self-assured with the academic success she was sure was in his future.

Looking on the positive side, Dr. Emily hoped that while he was at the rehab facility he would learn something from counseling about appropriate ways to cope with whatever was troubling him and had caused him to give up on life. Sometimes, all we can do is cope, she thought; but she hated that she had failed in getting Jud to tell her what had pushed him over the edge, and that bothered her. Would Jud be able to handle things on his own once he was back on campus? It would not be easy for him, she was sure. Perhaps the counselor had been able to guide him. Dr. Emily could only hope.

But for now, at least, it seemed the crisis had passed, and Jud appeared to be looking forward to returning to Merryvale. His participation in the Faire was uncertain, but Dr. Emily saw no reason why he shouldn't be able to play the part of the Clerk as planned and encouraged him to take part if he felt up to it. The Faire always lifted everyone's spirits, and she thought it would be the perfect way for him to transition back to the campus with a day of fun and revelry. She offered to see what could be done about putting a costume together for him from the Drama Department, just in case he was strong enough on the day of the Faire; and he seemed pleased with the idea. Over the years there had been numerous productions of Shakespeare's plays at the college, and she was sure something could be found that looked medieval.

She made a quick note in her daily planner about seeing to the costume for Jud and looked over the other things listed on her schedule for the day. Time was moving along a little too fast, she thought. It was hard to believe the Faire was only a week away. A meeting with Glenda to check on the progress the department was making with the details of the Faire would probably be a good idea, Dr. Emily realized. She was not about to leave anything to chance and assume that all the details for the big event had been taken care of.

In the past the Faire had always followed the same procedures from year to year, but there were always a million last-minute details to take care of. Various organizations on campus, the Foreign Language Club, for example, took the opportunity of having a large number of alumni back for a visit to schedule their own festivities. Other organizations arranged dinners and cocktail parties for the night before and were independent in their preparations. This, of course, was greatly appreciated by the hard-pressed members of the English Department and added a great deal to the festivities. Every year the crowds seem to grow larger, and what had started as a small production turned into a medieval extravaganza with booths set up for art work, crafts, and food.

The logistics of the procession seemed to be the most troublesome part of the planning. Early on the morning of the Faire, the participants in the production, all mounted on horseback, would be lined up in order of their appearance in Chaucer's *Prologue to the Canterbury Tales* and ride along a set route through campus, meeting at the middle of the Quad where a large stage had been built. The Drama Department, with its skill in set-building, was responsible for the construction, with very little variation from year to year. Built on several levels to suggest the appearance of the steps of Canterbury Cathedral, the end result was impressive. An image of the façade of the great cathedral was painted on several stage flats mounted on the back of the platform and was surprisingly realistic. With a little imagination the mood was set. Brightly colored pennants and flowers were used as decorations on the structure and the festive booths that covered the lawn. Voila! The campus was suddenly transformed into a Medieval Faire.

The Drama Department could always be counted on to provide actors to create the atmosphere of Chaucer's England. Students dressed in period costumes as minstrels and performers of various sorts would roam through the crowd. But the English Department would be responsible for the actual performance, with the Drama Department's collaboration, of course. The tradition was followed from year to year. Dr. Emily always read the part of the narrator of *The Prologue*, Chaucer's voice speaking over the centuries, the

Fourteenth Century to be exact. Dr. Bowen would read the part of Harry Bailey, the owner of the inn where the pilgrims gathered, the part which for so many years had been read by Dr. Stewart Stevens, now professor emeritus of the English Department.

But Dr. Emily's speaking part was by far the most demanding since the narrator describes in detail the appearance and personality of each character on the pilgrimage to Canterbury. Her reading of Middle English was flawless, but over the years it had been decided to use a more modern translation of *The Prologue* for the benefit of the general audience, and some editing of lengthy descriptions had taken place for brevity. Still, it would be a demanding day for Dr. Emily.

The actors' parts in the production were quite simple. They were required to remain on their horses, and as each one approached the stage they would stop briefly while the description of their character was read by Dr. Emily. They would smile and bow to the audience and then move on to be replaced by the next character. If there a certain amount of heckling from the crowd, so much the better; and in the spirit of the much later Elizabethan theatre, groundling behavior was tolerated and added to the fun and color of the production. Afterwards, there would be a very informal reception in the English Department; and later in the evening, private parties would be held in the town that would go on until the early hours.

Dr. Emily knew that coordination was the key to the success of the Faire; but she was beginning to wonder if Dr. Bowen was aware of what needed to be done. As the day of the Faire drew closer, he seemed to be either oblivious or uninterested in the production. As a result, she found herself taking on more responsibility than she had in past years. Not that she had any desire to take over; she simply wanted to make certain that all the little details had been covered and that the Faire was the success this year that it had always been.

She was trying to be diplomatic, if that was possible under the circumstances; and she was making an effort to not pass judgment on Dr. Bowen's leadership abilities at this point. After all, it must be rather intimidating, she thought, taking charge of an entire department where things had always been done a certain way under the leadership of Dr. Stevens. She certainly hoped that Dr. Bowen would settle into the department in time and develop a more take-charge attitude. If not, she was afraid much of the burden would fall on her shoulders.

But she was not discouraged. Dr. Emily always expected the best from everyone, that they would rise to the occasion, and that high standards would be upheld. After all, she expected no less from herself. If Dr. Bowen had offended several department members and had not seemed too interested in taking charge of the Faire and other departmental business, it was only a matter of time before he would understand what was expected, she thought. At least this is what she kept telling herself, but deep down she still felt a sense of foreboding and that something was not quite right about Dr. Basil Bowen, something that she couldn't quite understand.

In the meantime what a treasure Glenda had turned out to be. It was true; Dr. Emily had not exactly taken to her in the beginning. She wasn't sure exactly why she had felt that way other than that she thought Glenda would have been more suited to an office with more to do with the corporate world rather than the academic. Glenda seemed so worldly, and Dr. Emily had wondered if she would settle into an environment filled with stuffy academics and soon resign from sheer boredom.

Surprisingly, that had not happened, and Dr. Emily was happy that her reservations about Glenda had been unfounded. She had proven to be a very competent administrative assistant and was almost running the department single-handedly, especially since it seemed that Dr. Bowen was more than willing to turn over the day-to-day details to her. Glenda was thriving in her new position and was well on her way to becoming indispensable.

One Monday morning after her eight o'clock class, Dr. Emily stopped by the office to have a chat with Glenda and check on a few details that she had thought of over the weekend.

"Everything seems to be under control, Dr. Emily. All the parts have been assigned and costumes have been arranged. Everyone either made arrangements with the Drama Department to borrow a costume or they've made plans to rent one." Lowering her voice and looking around to make sure no one was in hearing distance, she continued, "Can you believe Elise Bowen got hers from the Alabama Shakespeare Theatre in Montgomery? How she managed that I can't imagine. I guess nothing we had was good enough for her." Glenda laughed; but although Dr. Emily smiled and nodded in agreement, she thought the comment revealed a deep dislike for the woman.

"Good for her! I'm sure we want everyone to be happy, Glenda; although there was really no need for her to go to that kind of expense. Surely a costume could have been found here on campus," Dr. Emily replied.

Glenda quickly changed the subject thinking that she had better temper her criticism of the department head's wife. "What about your costume, Dr. Emily? Do you have yours?"

"Yes, my dear. I always wear the same thing. It's a lovely emerald green gown with a high waist and long sleeves. The bodice is beautifully embroidered with fleurs de lis. The costumes are always so splendid, and the fact that everyone is on horseback makes it so much more authentic. It's such an important day for us." Dr. Emily couldn't help being caught up in the excitement.

"I'm curious. Has anyone ever fallen off?" Glenda inquired.

"Unfortunately, a few; but no one has ever been injured, I'm happy to report. Most of the spills were probably due to overindulgence the night before. The horses are very reliable. Rich Henry sees to that. He makes sure everyone is properly mounted and feels comfortable with their horse. I'm trying to remember. I think it's been a number of years since anyone has taken a spill."

"Well, don't speak too soon. I understand Elise Bowen plans to ride sidesaddle. Rich Henry is pretty hot about it. Refuses to saddle up for her, and the last I heard she insisted that if he wouldn't cooperate she would have Dr. Bowen do it. Then, of course, she threatened to report Rich to someone in the administration. She sure knows how to win friends and influence people," Glenda chuckled; but as her laughter died away, her face clearly reflected her obvious contempt for the woman. Too late, she realized she was perhaps revealing too much about her true feelings for Elise. She shifted a few papers around on her desk and smiled at Dr. Emily.

"I do hope Dr. Bowen can convince her to ride astride like everyone else. Personally my feet will be on the boards of the stage reading the words of dear Geoffrey Chaucer," Dr. Emily said.

Relieved that the subject had changed, Glenda said, "I can't wait, Dr. Emily. Everyone says you are the only person in the department who could manage to read the part, what with all that archaic language."

"Actually, I'll be reading a translation into more contemporary English, Glenda. A modern audience finds it much more enjoyable; but I prefer the language of Chaucer, the everyday language of London, the language of the streets in the 1390's. That explains much of Chaucer's popularity, you know. *The Canterbury Tales* was written for the common people and they adored it. It was the equivalent of today's number one on the New York Times Best Seller List. Sorry, I don't mean to lecture."

"Dr. Emily, I could listen to you all day. But I have a better idea. Why don't you pay me a little visit this afternoon after the office closes? I'll show you the costume I've put together for my part as the Wife of Bath and see if you approve. Then we can sit in my garden and have a cup of tea or a glass of wine. I really would like your opinion of my outfit."

"Shall we plan on around 5:30?" Dr. Emily asked. "We can go over a few remaining details."

"Perfect!"

Dr. Emily wondered if Glenda had actually read Chaucer's description of the Wife of Bath and how she was dressed before she started putting together her costume. Most people knew her as the sexy character and would perhaps try to dress in a provocative manner, and certainly Glenda struck her as the type of woman who would enjoy playing the part. Oh well, why shouldn't she enjoy herself? Taking her leave of Glenda, she smiled as she thought of her dressed in her costume on horseback. She would be perfect for the part no matter what she wore.

Her hose were of the choicest scarlet red,
Close gartered, and her shoes were soft and new.
Bold was her face, and fair, and red of hue.
She'd been respectable throughout her life,
With five churched husbands bringing joy and strife,
Not counting other company in youth;
But thereof there's no need to speak, in truth.
****

THE WIFE OF BATH
THE PROLOGUE TO THE CANTERBURY TALES
BY
GEOFFREY CHAUCER

Chapter 11

The Saturday morning of the Faire dawned cloudy and chilly for a spring morning in the Deep South. April could be cold one day and warm the next in Alabama; but no matter what the weather, the Faire would go on. Dr. Emily could remember only one year, about ten years earlier, when the weather had not cooperated. There had been heavy thunderstorms and hail that delayed the opening for two hours or more, but fortunately the sky had cleared enough later in the morning for the festivities to begin. Of course, there were some inconveniences with wet costumes, wet horses, tack, and mud; but everyone took it in good spirits and had a wonderful time.

Many people had commented that it was probably the most authentic Faire they had ever attended. Amazing what a little dirt and gloomy weather can do for atmosphere, and that particular Faire had been talked about for years to come. With the exception of that late start, not one Canterbury Faire had been called off for inclement weather. That was a remarkable record, she thought. After all, the show must go on!

On this cool spring morning Dr. Emily had been up since well before dawn going over the list of pilgrims and other last-minute details. In the past her only responsibility had been to arrive and read her part; but since Dr. Bowen still seemed unorganized, she thought it prudent to take up the slack. In all fairness perhaps Dr. Bowen had never been involved in a production of this scope. No doubt next year would be different. After all, some people were simply not good at event planning. Even at this late date she tried to give him the benefit of the doubt.

She hoped that at least this morning he could be relied upon to assemble the riders in the order of their appearance and be certain that he was in place at the front of the procession when the initial trumpet call was sounded for the Faire to begin. But, if not, she would be on hand at the stable to step in and see that all went smoothly.

Dr. Emily never left anything to chance, certainly not anything as important as the Faire. She admitted to herself, however, that this year she was looking forward to the day being over. She was feeling a little anxious. It's just a case of nerves, she thought. Not only was she worried about things going smoothly, but she had a growing concern about Dr. Bowen's ability to ride on horseback to the Quad and read his part.

For most of the week she thought he had looked unwell, rather drawn and pale, although he denied it when questioned about his health. Not only did he appear to be physically sick, but he seemed to be suffering from some deep-seated emotional conflict. He was jumpy and tense and most of the time seemed lost in his own thoughts. She had noticed his detachment during several of their meetings and wondered if he and his wife were having problems.

Dr. Emily had witnessed the tension between the pair on more than one occasion and wondered about the stability of the marriage. Elise seemed high strung and had not adapted well to the move from Virginia. She had certainly made no secret of being unhappy living in the small town in central Alabama and had not made any friends that Dr. Emily knew of. That's probably what's bothering him, she thought, or at least part of the problem; but she knew that wasn't the whole story. She thought he looked seriously ill as well.

"I must have picked up a virus," he said about mid-week. "I'm just not up to par." He had spent the early part of the week closed up in his office, only appearing when he had to give a lecture.

On Thursday afternoon he had seemed much improved and Dr. Emily breathed a sigh of relief. There could be a problem if Dr. Bowen was ill and couldn't take part in the Faire, but Dr. Emily had a backup plan. If that happened, she was sure Dr. Stevens would be happy to step in and read the part of Harry Bailey, the part he had played every year until his retirement. Actually, he had read the part so many times, Dr. Emily was sure he must know it by heart.

Harry Bailey, the host of the Tabard Inn where Chaucer's pilgrims had assembled to spend the night before setting out on their journey, would lead the procession to the stage. Although the part was small, it was important to the integrity of the performance. As Dr. Emily read the *Preamble*, he would dismount and join her on stage where he would remain as she read the description of each character as they approached. Dr. Bowen's spoken part would begin when Harry

Bailey suggested that each pilgrim tell a story on the way to Canterbury and back in order to provide entertainment on the journey.

Dr. Emily loved the convention used by Chaucer of a story within a story. It was a popular genre of the medieval period and opened a window to the life and culture of that long-ago time. So much could be learned from those stories told by a variety of people making their way toward Canterbury. Not for the first time Dr. Emily thought about what Chaucer would think about his *Prologue* written so long ago being performed as a play in a land that to him and everyone else in Europe was unknown, a land that had yet to be discovered. She was certain he would have been pleased that his stories were still providing entertainment in the "New World."

Dr. Emily came back to the present. Oh my! Where did the time go? Before she knew it, it was time to get ready for what she hoped would be another successful Canterbury Faire. After dressing in her costume, she went over the list of participants one last time. She was pleased that Jud had returned to campus a few days earlier and was looking forward to his part. Dr. Emily thought he had made remarkable progress in the last week or two; and although she was a bit concerned that he might have returned a bit too early to the rigors of college life, he had reassured her that he was anxious to resume his studies on campus in preparation for graduation. Dr. Emily was looking forward to seeing Jud in his role as the Clerk. It would make her day.

The day should begin in an orderly manner if all went as planned. The participants who would be on horseback had been told to report to the stables at nine o'clock. Once everyone was assembled and mounted on their horses they would line up in the order of their appearance in *The Prologue* and prepare for their journey through the campus to the Quad. They would depart from the stable and amble along the route, no more than a mile and a half in length, to the stage; but the pace would be slow since the riders would be following the uneven brick road. As much as everyone on campus loved the look of the brick streets, they were a menace to the unwary on foot, not to mention those on horseback. There was always the danger of one of the horses stumbling on the rough surface, so every reasonable precaution was taken.

As riders slowly departed the stable yard and the last pilgrim was out of sight, Rich Henry would no doubt breathe a sigh of relief, especially this year. Rich wasn't sure he could make it through another pilgrimage like this one. His retirement was long overdue, but every year the college had asked him to stay on for just a little longer, and for one reason or another he had agreed.

This year, however, had taxed his patience so much that he was seriously thinking about calling it quits. Elise Bowen and her unreasonable demands had been the reason for most of his stress. The woman seemed incapable of understanding that he was responsible for the safety of all the riders. He certainly didn't want to end his long association with the college over a sidesaddle, although it would serve her right if she couldn't manage it and took a spill, he thought.

Rich would be a happy man when Dr. Emily arrived to take charge. She had spoken with him earlier and assured him she would be there to handle any difficulties that might arise. Good, he had thought. He would turn Elise Bowen over to Dr. Emily. If anyone could handle the woman, Dr. Emily could. She had been kind and sympathetic as he explained about the sidesaddle and the problems it had created. He hated to add to her responsibilities, but he knew she would be able to deal with anything Elise Bowen could dish out. I don't know what this college would do without her, he thought.

Before the procession began, Dr. Emily would make sure everyone was in the right order in line. Under the circumstances, she wasn't leaving this crucial part of the planning in Dr. Bowen's hands, especially since he had seemed so ill during the week. After all the pilgrims were in their correct places in their order of appearance in *The Prologue,* Jess Thornton would drive her to the stage on the Quad in plenty of time to prepare for the arrival of the procession which always seemed to take forever. The pace was intentionally slow, allowing everyone along the route to have the opportunity to admire and heckle the pilgrims. It set the tone for the day and the spectators looked forward to the procession with great anticipation.

The brick walkways of the campus would be crowded with revelers. After the pilgrims had passed, those who had lined the walkways would follow along to join the large crowd already waiting for their first glimpse of the pilgrims. Led forward by members of the Drama Department decked out in medieval attire, each character would stop in front of the stage and be admired by the crowd. Then Dr. Emily's colorful description of each pilgrim on the long ago journey to Canterbury to the tomb of Saint Thomas à Becket would be flawlessly delivered.

Returning to the present, Dr. Emily heard a knock at her door. Glenda had offered to give her a ride to the stable, and here she was right on time. Max made a mad dash to the door, barking furiously. "Hush, Max! It's a friend." He stopped barking and trotted down the hallway still growling as he turned and watched Dr.

Emily from his post by the umbrella stand. Dr. Emily opened the door to Glenda, as Max made a hasty retreat to the kitchen with another low growl.

"What do you think?" Glenda asked as she spun around in the entrance hall giving Dr. Emily a 360-degree view of The Wife of Bath. And what a view it was! Glenda was a perfect re-creation of the notorious wife.

"Glenda, I'm overwhelmed with your costume! Your wimple looks absolutely authentic, and the overskirt is perfect with that blue gown, and that cape is absolutely stunning!"

"Wait until you see my hat! It's supposed to be a very wide one, you know. At least that's how Chaucer described it. Didn't he say it was as wide as her hips? Glenda burst into a hearty laugh. "I had such a time finding one large enough, so I finally found an old beach hat and used that as a base. Then with a little wire and velvet covering I managed to make one that is almost as wide!" Glenda's laughter rang out through the house. "I know my hips are rather womanly, but hopefully everyone will focus on my headgear and not pay too much attention to my bottom." Glenda was thoroughly enjoying herself. A low rumble could be heard from Max in the kitchen, followed by a sharp bark. Dr. Emily ignored him.

"Where on earth is this marvelous hat?" Dr. Emily laughed. She was greatly cheered by Glenda's arrival, and the worries that had haunted her most of the night and morning were soon dispelled. They both dissolved into laughter.

"On the back seat of the car. I couldn't get in to drive over here with it on my head. Someone will have to hand it to me once I'm on horseback. Oh, look at my red stockings!" She lifted her voluminous skirts, pointed her shapely foot, and did a little can-can kick." Both women burst into laughter again.

"Well, you certainly look the part," Dr. Emily said after catching her breath.

"I *am* perfect for the part, aren't I? I even have a little space between my two front teeth just like the real Wife of Bath. I read that the folks back then thought that was a sign of sexiness. Not that I've had five husbands like her. I can only claim three, and that was enough!" Glenda was in high spirits and the mood was contagious. Dr. Emily felt her spirits lift even more.

"Don't forget," Dr. Emily said, "according to Chaucer not only did she have the five husbands, but she had other paramours in her youth! Just imagine, I don't see how she found the time to go on pilgrimage, do you? And Chaucer wrote that she had traveled to the shrines of saints at many other holy places. Oh dear, look at the time. We will have to hurry to the stable before the crowd gets too heavy. Just give me a moment to get my briefcase and my script. Max, you be a good boy until I come back. Poor Max, doesn't like all this excitement," Dr. Emily laughed.

Glenda's outfit was sure to turn heads, Dr. Emily thought on their way to the car. She was already in character as the Wife of Bath, walking with a swing of her hips that made her skirts swish and lifting them well up her leg in order to show off her stockings. Her own outfit was the same one she had worn for years, but she loved it and looked forward to wearing the elegant dress. Only one part of the costume really bothered her. She found wearing the wimple very uncomfortable and couldn't understand why women of the Middle Ages put up with it. It completely covered her hair, ears and the tip of her chin, but worst of all seemed to stretch her skin; she felt like the corners of her eyes were being pulled back.

She had to admit it served one unintended purpose other than modesty. As she had dressed in her costume earlier that morning she looked at her reflection in the mirror and noticed that the wimple served as an instant face lift, pulling the skin tight and erasing the tiny lines around her eyes and on her cheeks. Still it seemed a high price to pay!

The wimple was a garment more suited to a climate colder than the South, and she knew from experience would be uncomfortably warm before the performance was over. Modesty was, of course, the main reason for the head covering and even nuns had worn a modified version well into the Twentieth Century. The liberation of women had made slow progress, she thought, since the days of Geoffrey Chaucer. No wonder so many women had embraced the Women's Movement with such enthusiasm a few decades ago. It was about time, she thought.

After some difficulty adjusting their costumes, Dr. Emily and Glenda finally got into the car and drove across the campus to the stable. Even at this early hour the crowds had already begun to gather along the route the pilgrims would take, in order to get an unobstructed front row view.

"The threat of rain and the cool temperature don't seem to have kept anyone at home," Glenda remarked.

"It never does, Dr. Emily replied. "Besides, the weather forecast calls for the sky to clear around mid-morning, just in time for the procession. Ah, here we are!"

The area around the stable was a hive of activity. Most of the riders were men since they represented the professions Chaucer described in the tales. Actually, there were only three women pilgrims: the Prioress, a Nun, and The Wife of Bath. With the arrival of Glenda the women riders were all accounted for. Elise had been one of the first to arrive and, as could be expected, was dressed to perfection in her role as the Prioress. She told everyone she could corner how she had made a special effort by leasing her costume from the Shakespeare Theatre in Montgomery. Most people seemed unimpressed. She certainly knew how to turn people off.

"Not likely," Glenda whispered to Dr. Emily. "I don't think the Shakespeare Theatre is in the habit of leasing costumes to just anyone who comes in off the street. I'll bet she got it from a costume rental in Montgomery or Birmingham."

"Most likely she had to send to New Orleans for it; but no matter, it certainly looks wonderful on her." Dr. Emily tried to be positive, but sometimes it was a struggle. "Good! I see Charlotte Stevens, Dr. Stevens' wife, has arrived. She will be playing the part of the Nun. A very small part in *The Prologue*, rather like an attendant to the Prioress." Perhaps she will be able to keep an eye on Elise.

Searching for her watch hidden under the long flowing sleeve of her dress, Dr. Emily noted that it was almost time for everyone to mount up. Peering around the groups of men laughing and talking she saw Rich Henry slowly making his way through the crowd toward her.

"We need to get the ladies ready first, Dr. Emily, and I'm probably going to need your help with that." His face was twisted into a frown. "I thought Dr. Bowen would be here by now and he'd be able to deal with his wife, but so far he hasn't shown up. She's still insisting she ride sidesaddle, and I refuse to permit it. I've saddled one of our gentlest mares for her. Maybe you can talk some sense into her. I can't get Mrs. Bowen to listen to reason!"

"I wonder what could be keeping him." Dr. Emily looked anxiously over the crowd.

"Probably trying to stay out of her way," Rich growled, jerking his head toward Elise Bowen.

"Here he is now," Glenda said, moving quickly toward him as he got out of his car.

"He doesn't look at all well," Dr. Emily said, turning to Rich. "I hope he can convince Elise to cooperate. I'm going to stay out of this dispute if you don't mind. After all, he is the department head and is supposed to be in charge."

Rich muttered something under his breath that Dr. Emily couldn't quite catch. She noticed Glenda had her hand under Dr. Bowen's arm as they walked toward

Elise. He looked deathly pale and seemed slightly unsteady on his feet. Glenda was perfect in the role of the earth mother, she observed; but then Glenda's role seemed to shift quickly to mediator as it became obvious that Basil and Elise were exchanging heated words. Basil's face became flushed and voices were raised.

Heads turned in their direction and curious onlookers moved toward the couple, no doubt out of curiosity or perhaps concern. Most people probably thought something serious had happened, but soon realized it was an argument between the couple that was causing the uproar. Those standing closest to the Bowens felt embarrassed for both of them and quickly moved away, their faces registering that they thought the whole thing in very poor taste. Marital arguments in public were few and far between on the campus of Merryvale College, although there were probably plenty behind closed doors.

Dr. Emily was appalled that Basil and Elise had chosen a public place to air their grievances and was so upset and distracted by their outburst that she didn't see Jud Sharp walking toward her. Dr. Emily jumped as Jud took her arm and said in a low voice, "Great pair aren't they?"

"Jud, you startled me!"

"I'm sorry," he said. "I just wanted to let you know I'm here. I hope you got my message. I wouldn't miss this for anything."

"My dear boy! Of course you must be here and take part. I know how long you've been looking forward to it. I'm so happy you're with us today." Dr. Emily's eyes brimmed with tears as she gazed into his face.

Jud took her hand and patted it in an attempt at comfort. His respect for Dr. Emily didn't need to be expressed in words. "Well, Dr. Emily, we look much happier than those two, that's for sure. I wonder what all of that is about. Someone should talk to them about how to behave in public. It doesn't reflect well on the department; that's for sure. But it really doesn't surprise me at all." Suddenly, Jud seemed subdued. "Oh well, let's get on with the show!" He looked at Dr. Emily and forced a smile.

Next morning, when the day began to spring,
Up rose our host, and acting as our cock,
He gathered us together in a flock
And forth we rode, a jog-trot being the pace,
Until we reached St. Thomas' watering-place.
****

THE HOST
THE PROLOGUE OF THE CANTERBURY TALES
BY
GEOFFREY CHAUCER.

Chapter 12

"Elise, you're making a spectacle of yourself! For god's sake, get on the horse and shut up! Why do you have to make an issue of something as trivial as a saddle?" Basil hissed.

"Don't you dare talk to me that way, Basil! I swear I hate you almost as much as I hate this place."

The other pilgrims moved as far away as possible, but still those closest to the couple could easily hear their heated exchange and most thought the whole episode simply appalling. The department head and his wife were expected to set a certain tone, and they had certainly failed today! Looks were exchanged and disgust was clearly visible on several faces.

Rich Henry led Elise's horse to her side and handed her the bridle. He had chosen one of the oldest mares in the stable, one they normally used for inexperienced riders. "Madame," he smirked, "Your mount awaits!"

Elise gave Rich a cutting look as she turned to Basil. "Would you look at the nag he expects me to ride?" Realizing it was a losing battle, she gave up the argument and got ready to mount the gentle mare Rich held for her.

"Don't just stand there, Basil. Give me a leg up," she shrilled in a petulant voice that carried to the pilgrims unsuccessfully trying to ignore the unpleasant scene.

Ignoring her demand, Basil turned and walked away, his pale face mottled with the heat of the argument. He still looked seriously ill. Glenda, who had stepped aside during their rather volatile argument, reached his side before anyone else.

"You look like you need to be home in bed, Dr. Bowen," Glenda whispered. "Let me help you." She led him a short distance away from the crowd of pilgrims.

Most of the onlookers, bored by now with the unaccustomed public drama, turned away from the scene and began to mount up.

Basil looked at Glenda and smiled weakly. "Thank you, for being so kind. By the way, your costume is perfect for the Wife of Bath. Sorry about that scene with Elise." They stood together talking for a few moments before Glenda turned back toward the participants with a swirl of her long cape.

"If you insist on riding, Dr. Bowen, let's try to enjoy the day, shall we? Oh, look. There's Dr. Goldman!" She put her arm under his and began to steer him over to where Dr. Emily was standing with Jud Sharp. Jud, watching the two as they approached, turned and left hurriedly without another word to Dr. Emily.

"Was that Jud dashing off?" Glenda asked.

Dr. Emily nodded. "Yes, that was Jud. He's looking forward to the Faire. Dr. Bowen, you don't look at all well. Do you think you should ride?" Her concern was genuine.

"Oh, yes, Dr. Goldman. I'll take my place at the head of the procession of pilgrims. Never fear." He gave a slight shudder as if gripped by a sudden pain and rubbed his hand across his abdomen. "Elise's cooking no doubt. I think she's trying to poison me." He smiled weakly and his joke fell flat. Neither Glenda nor Dr. Emily cracked a smile. "Seriously, I haven't been well all week, as you both know. I think it must be a touch of the stomach flu, but I'll not let the department down. I'll get through this. All I have to do is sit on my horse and ride to the Quad. Thank goodness I only have a small part to read."

"If you're sure you're up to it. Dr. Stewart is dressed in costume and can easily fill in for you," Dr. Emily said.

"No, no! I won't hear of it. Stiff upper lip and all that!" Basil reached into his pocket and took out a flask and took a deep drink. "That should get me through the morning," he said.

Dr. Emily's concern for Dr. Bowen was increasing by the minute, but her attention shifted momentarily to her protégé. "Now where did Jud get off too? I wanted to tell him to be sure and take his time when he stops in front of the stage. I want everyone to get a good look at his costume. I offered to find something for him, but he made the entire outfit himself. So authentic looking."

At the mention of Jud Sharp's name, a look flashed across Dr. Bowen's face that puzzled Dr. Emily. For a moment, she thought it was a combination of guilt and fear. The man looked so ill, she thought. Perhaps he was simply reliving the unfortunate altercation with his wife.

Rich Henry approached the group. "Better have everyone mount up, Dr. Emily. Time to get started."

"Thank you, Rich. What would we do without you?"

Dr. Emily raised her clear high voice enough to be heard over the colorful group of pilgrims all dressed to perfection as their character in *The Prologue*. "Get ready to line up, everyone. First, Dr. Bowen as the Host, then the Knight, and the Squire."

Those who were not already on horseback quickly mounted, with some needing the assistance of Rich Henry and a few of his volunteers. Many expert riders had difficulty in dealing with their costumes as they were mounting the horses and needed a leg up, especially the men portraying members of the church with their long robes. Dr. Bowen nodded at Dr. Emily and made his way unsteadily to his horse, one he had ridden and enjoyed on several visits to the stable. He swung expertly into the saddle and rode out of the stable yard and stopped, waiting for the others to line up behind him.

Dr. Emily continued calling out the names of the twenty-nine pilgrims in the order of their appearance in Chaucer's wonderful tale. Not for the first time she regretted the necessity of using a modern translation and the shortening of many of the characters' colorful descriptions, but she knew it was necessary to play to the audience. After all, they were not all scholars of Medieval English. Besides, it would have been a daunting task to read the entire *Prologue* aloud.

Just as Dr. Emily read out the name of the Pardoner, the final pilgrim, Jess Thornton appeared to drive her to the Quad so she could take her place on the stage.

"Thank you, Jess. I can always depend on you to be on time," she said as she settled the folds of her long gown around her feet.

"There seems to be a big crowd this year, Dr. Emily," he said as he wheeled the police car around the line of horses and drove as fast as safety permitted along the bumpy brick drive towards the middle of campus. "And it looks like the weather is going to cooperate. I thought I saw a little patch of blue sky a moment ago."

"Just so it doesn't rain, Jess. Actually, I'm enjoying the cooler temperature this year. Remember year before last when it was so warm?"

'Indeed I do, Dr. Emily. Everyone was burning up in those costumes and developed a great thirst for refreshments. It took all of my patience to see that everyone stayed safe, students and grownups alike. Nearly wore me out. Well, here we are, Madame Chaucer," he said with a laugh.

Dr. Emily smiled at him and patted his hand. "You were right, Jess. I see a little patch of cerulean peeking through the clouds!"

"That must be blue," he grinned.

Untangling herself from the gown, she got out of the police car and greeted the revelers waiting around the stage for the production to begin. The students from the Drama Department were on hand to assist her and for crowd control, making sure everyone was far enough back from the stage to allow the safe passage of the horses in front of the faux stone steps, painted to suggest those of the great Cathedral of Canterbury.

A young man dressed as a court jester gave Dr. Emily a low bow and, leaping to her side, helped her up to the stage. Everyone was certainly in high spirits, she thought, as she caught her breath and arranged her script on her podium. She was thankful that someone had been thoughtful enough to provide a pitcher of water and a glass for her, and as she poured herself a drink she heard the cheers far away in the distance as the journey to Canterbury began. A thrill of excitement ran up her spine.

Dr. Emily thought about all the years she had taught her advanced class on the works of Geoffrey Chaucer and how much she loved the subject matter. How blessed she was to be able to teach something that she really loved and that she never grew tired of sharing with students. The historical background so necessary to an understanding of *The Canterbury Tales* was equally fascinating, she thought.

What a lesson it taught, even today. One had to be very careful about language. When King Henry II of England had become frustrated with his Archbishop of Canterbury, he made the mistake of saying what he thought; or at least that's the story that has been handed down over the centuries. Thinking aloud, he had said, "Will no one rid me of this turbulent priest?" Four of his men had hastened to do just that. Taking him at his word, they murdered his Archbishop and one-time friend, Thomas, in the great Cathedral of Canterbury as he was saying mass or in silent prayer. The story varies in the telling.

King Henry was overcome with guilt, was almost excommunicated by the Pope, and did public penance for the murder by allowing monks to publically whip him as he walked barefoot to the Cathedral. Within two years Becket was declared a saint and pilgrims traveled to pray at his tomb. And then 220 years later, or there about, Chaucer wrote the timeless *Canterbury Tales*. Language was powerful, Dr. Emily reflected, and could change the course of history.

She was brought back to the present with the sounding of a trumpet which signified the procession's approach to "Canterbury." The pace seemed rather slow this year. It was normally a thirty or forty-minute ride at a sedate walk from the stables to the Quad. No doubt the larger crowd this year had slowed them down, and care had to be taken on the brick pavement once the procession made its way to the campus proper. Minstrels had serenaded the crowd, along with other entertainment provided by jesters and jugglers as everyone waited for the arrival of the pilgrims.

From her elevated position on stage, Dr. Emily could just make out the fancy headgear of the riders as they made their way through the crowds. Not much longer, she thought. They would stop before they had reached the stage for a few minutes in order to give her time to read Chaucer's introduction, explaining the purpose of the journey and giving details about the reason for the pilgrimage. It was almost time for her to begin her reading.

She saw the procession stop and could see that several of the drama students were at the head of the procession to make certain that the first pilgrim, Dr. Bowen, approached the stage at the proper time and to help him dismount from his horse. He would then join her on the stage. Later he would read the part of Harry Bailey, the Innkeeper, which explained how the stories would be told as the pilgrims journeyed to Canterbury. She must remember to thank each and every one of the drama students. Two young men in period costumes stood on each side of Dr. Bowen's horse holding the bridle. Out of the corner of her eye, Dr. Emily thought she saw him sway slightly in the saddle.

It was time to begin. A final trumpet sounded and Dr. Emily began to read:

When April with his showers sweet with fruit
The drought of March has pierced unto the root
And bathed each vein with liquor that has power
To generate therein and sire the flower;
When Zephyr also has, with his sweet breath,
Quickened again, in every holt and heath,
The tender shoots and buds, and the young sun
Into the Ram one half his course has run,
And many little birds make melody
That sleep through all the night with open eye
(So Nature pricks them on to ramp and rage)-
Then do folk long to go on pilgrimage,
And palmers to go seeking out strange strands,
To distant shrines well known in sundry lands.
And specially from every shire's end
Of England they to Canterbury wend,
The holy blessed martyr there to seek
Who helped them when they lay so ill and weak.

Dr. Emily's clear sweet voice rang out over the assembled throng. The audience was silent, listening respectfully to the opening lines of Chaucer's great work, no doubt saving their jests and jokes until each character approached the stage. Ironically, Dr. Emily had just read the line about paying homage to the blessed saint who had helped the pilgrims when they had been so ill and weak, when she caught a sudden movement in the line of pilgrims from the corner of her eye. She glanced quickly to her left just in time to see Dr. Bowen slump slightly and, as if in slow motion, slide from the saddle and hit the ground with a sickening thump.

Those nearest the stage had a clear view of Dr. Bowen as he fell from his horse, and there was an audible gasp as the crowd realized he had been suddenly stricken down. Fortunately, Jess Thornton was near the steps to the stage and rushed to Dr. Bowen's side, reaching for his radio as he ran. Kneeling in the grass next to the doctor he gently rolled him over onto his back on the soft grass and quickly checked his pulse and respiration. Dr. Bowen's eyes were wide open staring at the sky as the clouds broke overhead.

Jess Thornton's authoritative voice could be heard over the crowd. "Get back everyone. Give him some air, please!" The serious tone of his voice created an immediate response and the crowd backed up a few feet. "I need an ambulance and paramedics at the college ASAP," he barked into the radio. "This is Thornton. I'm in front of the stage on the Quad. Send me some extra officers to help with the crowd." Jess had assessed the gravity of the situation almost immediately and called for additional officers from the county.

Fourth in the line of pilgrims, behind the Knight, Squire, and Yoeman, Elise Bowen had been looking in the other direction when Basil fell. She was still stewing about the confrontation with Rich Henry, and it was a moment or two before she realized that Dr. Goldman had stopped reading and all eyes had turned from the stage and were focused on the pilgrims. Dr. David Cunningham, Professor of Music, in his role as the Knight was directly behind Basil's horse. Not realizing the seriousness of Basil's condition, he turned in his saddle and passed word back to Elise that Basil had taken a fall.

Serves him right, she thought; but her face soon registered concern at the silence that had fallen over the crowd. One of the student volunteers appeared at her side and helped her dismount, taking the reins of her horse. Barely containing her annoyance, she walked briskly toward the small group kneeling on the ground around her husband. The wail of a siren could be heard in the distance and the crowd instinctively began to make way for the emergency responders.

Looking around her, Elise was struck again by the silence. Only a moment before there had been smiles and a festive atmosphere; but now people spoke in whispers, if at all; and it began to occur to her that Basil might be seriously hurt. How could he have fallen off his horse, she wondered? He was an excellent rider. They had reined in the horses and were waiting for the signal from Dr. Emily for Basil to join her at the stage before they all rode forward and had their turn in the limelight. He must have tried to dismount and had trouble with the long tunic that was part of his costume, or perhaps his cloak had caught on the saddle. On second thought, she realized, he was probably drunk. She had noticed he had been sipping from a flask as they rode across campus. Fool, she thought!

It was only when she reached the group of men huddled around Basil that she realized it was more than alcohol. She looked down at her husband and with a shock saw that he was having a seizure as he lay helpless on the grass at her feet. Jess Thornton and another man were holding him as his limbs thrashed violently and were suddenly still. Elise turned her head away from him and began to scream.

A knight there was, and he a worthy man,
Who, from the moment that he first began
To ride about the world, loved chivalry,
Truth, honour, freedom and all courtesy.
****

THE KNIGHT
THE PROLOGUE TO THE CANTERBURY TALES
BY
GEOFFREY CHAUCER

Chapter 13

Glenda stopped the car in front of her small house and turned to Dr. Emily. "Let's go inside and make some tea and then sit in the garden for a while before I take you home. It's been a difficult day for all of us. I can't imagine how you were able to continue with the reading after Dr. Bowen took sick."

"That's very thoughtful of you, Glenda. I must admit, the idea of going home to an empty house doesn't appeal to me right now. Of course, Max will be waiting faithfully, bless his heart. It was a good thing Dr. Stevens was on hand to take Basil's part, and his dear wife did a fine job filling in for Elise as the Prioress. I don't believe many people noticed that her costume was all wrong and that I skipped over the nun. There's really no description of her anyway, just a companion of the Prioress. I suppose it went as well as it could under the circumstances; and, of course, Elise would be expected to accompany her husband to the hospital. No one would have expected her to stay, with Basil being so ill."

"You can congratulate yourself, Dr. Emily, for being a real trooper. I checked my watch and there was only about a 30-minute delay. The horses got a little restive, of course; but the crowd was quiet, and you did a wonderful job of reassuring everyone that Dr. Bowen would be taken care of and that he would have wanted the production to go on as planned. You do know how to handle a crowd."

"It's hard to know what to do in a situation like that, Glenda. I hope we did the right thing. So many people would have been disappointed if we had cancelled the Faire, and just think about all the hard work that would have gone to waste. I'm certain Dr. Bowen would have wanted us to carry on. Still, worry about him did cast a pall over the production."

She has a beautiful yard, Dr. Emily thought as they walked toward Glenda's front door. "Your home is charming, Glenda. With the landscaping you did last fall it looks like a cottage in England. I've always liked this street. It's close to campus, but far enough away to feel a little bit removed, if you understand what I mean."

"Oh, I do understand, Dr. Emily. There's something about Merryvale College. It doesn't take long for it to become your whole life."

"It certainly has been mine," Dr. Emily said with a touch of melancholy in her voice.

"Don't worry, Dr. Emily. Everything will be all right."

Once inside, Glenda slipped off several of the outer layers of her costume and then busied herself making tea and setting out a silver tray with cups and saucers. When the water boiled and the tea was made, she picked up the tray and moved toward the door leading from the kitchen into the back garden. "Come out this way, Dr. Emily. You were here not too long ago, but I think you'll notice the difference in the kitchen garden since you were here. If you're too warm in all your finery, I'll be happy to let you borrow something to slip on."

"Don't bother, Glenda. I'm thankful for this April cool snap and feel quite comfortable. Actually, I love any excuse to dress up, especially in period costume, and this dress is cut for comfort. Of course I had to get out of that wimple as soon as possible. Poor women, I don't understand how they ever came up with that fashion. It probably had something to do with the men not wanting the women to flaunt their lovely locks. Forgive me, Glenda. I can't seem to stop thinking about the past. History and literature have been my life, after all."

She settled herself on an elaborately scrolled wrought iron chair made comfortable with thick, all weather cushions, one of a matched set with a glass-topped table. Dr. Emily slowly began to relax and gaze around the garden.

"Oh, yes, so many more blooms than when I was here before. You are a skilled landscaper, I see. A master gardener. I love how you have the taller plants growing against the back wall and the others arranged by size to show them off. Beautifully done, Glenda; and how convenient to have your herbs right here near the kitchen door. During the Medieval period most houses had extensive kitchen gardens, you know. So much better than buying at grocery stores like we do today." Dr. Emily felt that she was beginning to ramble and recognized the fatigue that was beginning to set in after the stress and shock of the morning.

"Thank you, Dr. Emily. My garden is my refuge. I can escape here and nothing really bothers me when I'm digging in the dirt." She gave a short laugh. "Therapy, I call it. Without having to pay for it or bare your soul to a stranger. Just the cost of plants and a few seeds."

Dr. Emily sipped her tea. "Jess Thornton must have accompanied the ambulance to the hospital. I'm a little surprised he didn't come back to the Faire, but I suppose he had plenty of men on duty and probably decided we could spare him. Someone needed to stay with Elise, and I don't believe anyone went with her."

"She hasn't made too many friends since she's been here," Glenda said. "It's strange, I wasn't aware that Dr. Bowen had seizures. Seems like we should have been told about any medical problems he might have, don't you agree?"

"Actually, we really know very little about him, Glenda. He has that famous British reserve everyone talks about, so I suppose it will take us a little more time to get to know him. I do wonder how he is doing. He looked so ill that I can't help but worry." Dr. Emily took a sip of her tea and returned the cup to the table with a slightly unsteady hand. "I thought we would have heard something by now. It must be close to noon."

"Actually it is well past one. I sent Jess Thornton a text before we left the Quad and told him you were with me and that we would be here at my house. Maybe he'll let us know something before long."

Dr. Emily gave Glenda a knowing look and smiled with approval.

"Well, yes I have been seeing him from time to time. A girl gets lonely, you know."

"Indeed, I do know," Dr. Emily replied.

Glenda was just about to get up enough nerve to ask Dr. Emily a few personal questions about her life and why she had never married when Jess walked through the garden gate. His face was grim and both women immediately knew by his expression that the news was not good.

"He died about an hour ago," he said as gently as possible. He sat down next to Glenda as she put her hand to her mouth and the color drained from her face. "I know it's a shock to you both." He patted Glenda's hand and looked at Dr. Emily with concern. She had lost an important member of her academic community, and he had been worried about breaking the news to her. It had only been a few weeks since she had been shocked by Jud's suicide attempt, and he knew she had not fully recovered from almost losing the boy. With Dr. Bowen's death following so soon and the stress of the Faire, his concern for her health was at the forefront of his mind and written on his face. He had to keep reminding himself that she was no longer young, although he rarely thought about her age. He was afraid he had not handled it well, had just blurted it out, rather than leading up to the news in a gentle manner. He knew all about her tender heart and that there would be no easy way to tell her, but he cursed himself for not handling it better.

Dr. Emily felt weak and her hand trembled as she placed her tea cup on the table. Her blue eyes were blurred with tears, but her inquiring mind was already at work. "What was the cause of death, Jess?"

She may have a tender heart, but she always went straight to the crux of the matter, Jess thought. "The doctors aren't sure. From what I gathered at the hospital, the symptoms were not consistent with a heart attack. Since he had a seizure and a second one in the ER, they suspect it is something more complicated. He had no history of heart problems according to Elise; and although they aren't ruling out an attack, they think something else must have caused his death. One of the doctors thought it might be some sort of paralysis similar to a stroke. We won't know anything until after the autopsy and all the lab reports are reviewed."

"How is Elise?" Dr. Emily asked.

"Shocked, of course. I don't think it's hit her yet. I did hear that some of her people are flying in from Virginia to be with her."

"Where is she now? The poor woman doesn't need to be alone until her family can arrive and help her."

Jess shook his head. "She was at the hospital, of course. I had a few words with her after the doctors told us they hadn't been able to do anything to save him. I left her with the hospital chaplain while I spoke with the attending physician; but by the time I'd finished asking a few questions, I was told she had left. She must have followed the ambulance to the hospital in her car; but now that I think about it, I don't remember seeing it in the ER parking lot. I'm assuming she must have driven herself home. I agree with you, Dr. Emily. Someone should have been with her; but, unfortunately, she seems to have little need for any of us."

"She's probably in shock, poor thing," Dr. Emily said. "I imagine she's gone back to her house. Someone should check on her. She must feel terrible."

"It's no secret she and Basil had a few words before the procession began," Glenda said. "I couldn't help but overhear, probably along with everyone else. The last words she said to him were, 'I hate you, Basil!' She must feel pretty bad about that."

"And what about Jud?" Dr. Emily said with a start. "We mustn't forget about him. He was in the procession of pilgrims and seemed to be calm as I read the description of his character, even though I'm sure he'd been close enough to see Dr. Bowen fall. By the way, he was absolutely perfect in the role. He was the absolute image of the Clerk." Dr. Emily sighed and shook her head sadly. "I have the feeling that he's another one who doesn't need to be alone. You don't suppose he left right afterwards, do you? I didn't see him after he rode past the stage."

"I don't remember seeing him either." Glenda remarked with a slight frown.

"Someone needs to make sure all is well with that young man," Dr. Emily said with a glance toward Jess. "He's been through a difficult time and now to have this happen. Of course, he may not have heard yet that Dr. Bowen is dead. It would be a shock to any young person who has so recently faced death himself." Dr. Emily sighed. "See if you can find him, Jess, and bring him to my house."

"I'll do that Dr. Emily, after I run you home and check on Mrs. Bowen."

"I don't know what we would do without you."

"Neither do I," Glenda purred.

Of study too he most care and heed.
Not one word spoke he more than was his need,
And that was spoke in form and reverence,
And short and quick and full of high sentence.
****

THE CLERK
THE PROLOGUE TO THE CANTERBUY TALES
BY
GEOFFREY CHAUCER

Chapter 14

The cool spring days of April slipped by all too soon. Before Dr. Emily could catch her breath from the Faire and the unfortunate events surrounding it, the month was gone. May, that month the academic world longs for during the winter and early spring term, was almost upon them. With graduation only a few weeks away, Dr. Stevens had agreed to temporarily fill in as department head until a replacement for Dr. Bowen could be found. Dr. Emily was greatly relieved. If the truth were known, she had been afraid the Dean would ask her to step in and lead the department. She shuddered at the thought.

Fortunately, Dr. Stevens was more than willing to take over Dr. Bowen's classes as well, and as a result the students lost very little in terms of their semester work. After years of running the department, he simply slipped back into his role as department head, accompanied by sighs of relief from everyone, his wife included. Actually, Dr. Stevens had found retirement rather tedious; and since he was in excellent health, he was happy to be back in his element. With the academic concerns taken care of and graduation ceremonies looming on the horizon, Merryvale College's English Department was returning to normal; but it was not to last.

Haunted by recent events, Dr. Emily found it difficult to settle back into a routine; and the afternoons normally set aside for her own study and research were not as enjoyable as they once had been. Instead of working on the paper she planned to submit to a conference on Anglo-Saxon Literature scheduled at her alma mater for later in the year, she sat with her hands folded in contemplation. Rather than getting on with her research, she gazed out of the lovely old window in her office watching students come and go to class and going over the events that had led up to the Faire and Dr. Bowen's tragic death. Every detail of the day was replayed in her memory, but it was the revelations Jud had made to her on the afternoon of Dr. Bowen's death that kept her going back over each detail in the hope that something would be revealed to her. She simply couldn't stop reliving it.

On the afternoon of the Faire, after taking their leave of Glenda, Jess Thornton had escorted Dr. Emily back to her house. True to his word, he had tracked down Jud in his dorm room and told him of Dr. Bowen's death and suggested that it might be a good idea to sit with Dr. Emily for the rest of the afternoon.

"She's not a young woman, Jud; and when I left her, she was upset," Jess confided.

Jud seemed calm but withdrawn. Jess had expected him to be shocked or at least express some emotion when he learned of his professor's death, but he had not seemed at all surprised. He nodded in agreement with Jess's suggestion about spending time with Dr. Emily and immediately began to gather some books together to put in his backpack.

"Yes, that would be a good idea," he replied. "I'm indebted to Dr. Goldman, you know. She's been very understanding and has helped me a great deal since I've been here. It's the least I can do. I hope she's not too upset."

"Thanks, Jud. I would appreciate it if you would keep an eye on her this afternoon. I don't want her to be alone." Actually, Jess felt a great deal better with both of them together until things settled down.

In Jess's opinion Jud Sharp was still a deeply troubled young man, and he hoped that the visit with Dr. Emily would in some way help them both. Not that he was really worried about Dr. Emily. He knew from experience that she was much tougher than she looked. In the past she had been invaluable to the local police and on more than one occasion had help resolve issues on campus that could have developed into something much more serious without her tact and compassion. More than one foolish undergraduate had benefited from her counseling. He hoped that she would be able to talk to Jud and find out the real reason behind his attempted suicide. Jess was not buying the explanation of depression and stress. He felt there was much more to it than that, but so far had been unable to come up with any answers.

When they arrived at Dr. Emily's house, she greeted them with warmth and seemed grateful for Jud's company. Max looked at them suspiciously but was well-mannered enough not to bark.

"Come in, Jud. Let's go into my study. We can be more comfortable in there. Jess, I hope you can stay."

"Sorry, Dr. Emily. Still too much to do, I'm afraid. I need to tie up a few loose ends before I can relax. I'll check back with you this evening to make sure you're feeling all right."

"Oh, there's no need for that, Jess. I'll be fine now that I have Jud to keep me company for the rest of the afternoon. Then I'm sure he has some studying or perhaps something more enjoyable for a Saturday night. I'm sure the Faire is still in full swing and there will be plenty of things to do."

"I can't imagine anything better than spending time with you, Dr. Goldman," Jud responded.

"There, you see. I'm all set for the afternoon. Run along now, Jess. Don't let me keep you from your duties."

As Jess let himself out, he heard Dr. Emily suggesting that Jud make some tea and serve it in the study. Now they would have the time and privacy to have a serious conversation; and perhaps Dr. Emily could find out what was really at the heart of Jud's problem, Jess thought. For some reason he could not shake off the idea that Jud's unhappiness had some connection with Dr. Bowen. Not to his death, of course, but he was aware of the discontent and outright anger of some of the faculty members in the English Department concerning what looked like heavy-handedness on Dr. Bowen's part. Jess wondered if some of the students had felt the same way. Certainly,

Dr. Bowen had not been tactful with his new faculty, and it was not unheard of for students to suffer at the hands of professors on an ego trip or obsessed with their own agenda.

Jud found his way around Dr. Emily's well organized kitchen with little difficulty and before long had made tea and brought it to her cozy home office.

"I love this room," Jud said as he slumped down into one of the comfortable arm chairs. His eyes traveled over the floor-to-ceiling bookcases that contained her collection of everything from rare books on Old English to more contemporary writers. On either side of a small fireplace comfortable chairs were placed, one of which he occupied. Near the window that looked out on her patch of garden was a small desk with a flat-screen monitor and keyboard. Dr. Emily might seem to be from another age, but she had embraced the wonders of technology with enthusiasm.

She moved from behind her desk and sat in the arm chair opposite Jud. With the tea tray on a small table between them in front of the fireplace, they were ready to settle in for a long visit. Dr. Emily reached across to the table and picked up a remote control. Suddenly a cheerful flame glowed from the gas logs in the grate.

"Don't you love it?" Dr. Emily laughed. "Imagine. A remote control fire! My dear Mother would have been astonished. And so convenient—these old houses with high ceilings tend to be chilly, especially in the afternoon. Isn't it wonderful to be able to have a fire without all the mess?"

"We do seem to be having a rather chilly spring. It'll be warm weather soon, and we'll long for the cool air," Jud replied. "Yes, I do love this room," he said again. "I would love to have a place like this, a proper library."

"Well, there's no reason why you shouldn't. When you finish your advanced studies, I fully expect you to have a position at a college or university and then you can establish your own library or study in your own house."

"I don't expect that will happen now, Dr. Goldman." Dr. Emily looked at Jud in surprise. "Why ever not? Look, Jud, I know you're supposed to be here to cheer me up; and I know Jess Thornton has a tendency to worry about me and thinks that what happened today has me terribly upset. I also know that he thinks that I don't need to be alone. That's nonsense. Of course Dr. Bowen's death is upsetting. I don't mean to suggest that it isn't; but you must know, dear boy, that I've been terribly concerned about you also. Now you tell me that you've lost your hope for an academic career! What on earth is going on? The only way I'm going to feel better is for you to tell me what precipitated your attempt to take your life. Be honest with me, Jud. We really haven't had an opportunity to talk since you came back to campus. What you tell me will be held in strictest confidence."

"I know I can trust you, Dr. Goldman. I've never doubted you, please believe that; but you have to understand. I lost faith in everything, more or less lost my mind for a period of time; and I certainly lost hope. More lost hope than anything else, I guess. Now that he's dead, I suppose it doesn't really matter." He leaned forward in his chair and with both elbows on his knees covered his face with his hands.

"What happened, Jud? It has something to do with Dr. Bowen, doesn't it?"

"Yes," he said, reluctantly. "It does. I'm afraid this is going to shock you, Dr. Goldman."

"Jud, there is nothing you can tell me that will shock me. You may think that I've led a fairly sheltered life, but remember I'm a scholar of literature and history. I know all about man's inhumanity to man."

"You're the smartest person I've ever met, Dr. Goldman. I didn't mean to insinuate that you aren't aware of the way of the world. I didn't mean to suggest..." his voice trailed off. "This is hard for me to talk about; but, you see, Dr. Bowen made advances toward me. They were of a sexual nature, Dr.

Goldman." Jud drew a deep breath before he continued. "I rejected him, and from that point on he made my life almost unbearable. I guess he thought I wouldn't tell anyone about it. He was right, of course; I didn't want to jeopardize my chance for graduate school."

"I had begun to suspect it was something like that. When did this happen, Jud?"

"The first time was during the second week of October. If you remember, I was taking his advanced class on Shakespeare's history plays. There was one other time a few weeks after that. I told him to leave me alone. He acted so superior. Then he actually laughed at me, said I was an inexperienced boy, and some other things I'd rather not tell you!" Jud's face flushed, hot with anger. "I could have overlooked it if there had only been the one time, I guess. When it happened again, I wanted to put a stop to it, but I didn't know how. It was sexual harassment after all."

Dr. Emily spoke calmly, but she could feel her anger rising. "I can imagine that must have been very upsetting for you, Jud. Did you think about reporting the incident to someone?"

"No, no! I couldn't have done that. He would have denied it; and besides, I'm just a student with no money, no influence. Don't you see, he would have been believed? He would have made up something; turned it around to make it look like I was the one in the wrong, that I was lying."

"Yes, I suppose he would have. It's unbelievable. He had only been here a few months, in a position of trust. You would think he would have been on his best behavior."

Dr. Emily shook her head and was quiet for a few minutes. This must be why I have felt so uneasy about the department, she thought.

"Our tea is cold," she said, looking at Jud and noticing the pallor of his skin. It must have taken courage for him to talk about this, and now he was realizing the enormity of what he had just told her. Merryvale College has a strict code of professional behavior, and fraternization between students and faculty is not encouraged; but she slowly began to sense that there was much more to this than sexual harassment.

"I'll make a fresh pot of tea and some sandwiches. I don't know about you, but I can't remember having lunch, and I just realized we need some nourishment."

Max followed Dr. Emily into her tidy kitchen, and sat expectantly, watching his mistress's every move. He rarely let her out of his sight. He cocked his head from one side to the other and looked into the study, not entirely certain about this young man that was taking up so much of his mistress's time.

As she busied herself in the kitchen, Jud paced the floor in the library. He had no idea what she would think about the rest of the betrayal. That's how he thought of it, a betrayal. She would know what to do; that, he believed with certainty. He realized that he had been very foolish not to have come to her before things got so far out of hand. Of course it was much easier to talk about now that the man was dead. He would tell Dr. Goldman the whole story, and that would be the end of it. Perhaps then he would be able to put it behind him.

"Here we are. Let's drink our tea and eat. We can continue to talk this over when we've regained our strength." Max followed her into the study and with a loud sign sat at Dr. Emily's feet waiting for a treat. She had remembered to put one of his favorite dog biscuits on the tray. Content with the attention and confident he had not been replaced in her affection by this young man, he settled down for a nap.

Once they had devoured every crumb and both had downed two cups of strong sweet tea, Dr. Emily felt fortified enough to ask Jud a few more questions about the events that led up to his suicide attempt. After the revelations Jud had just made, there were still several things that she simply could not understand. She was a good judge of character and human nature and past events had proven her correct in this self-analysis, she thought. Now, she was wondering why a sexual advance from another man, granted, one in a position of trust, would have been taken so seriously by this young man sitting across from her. In her day she supposed it would have been shocking, but today with everything so out in the open she doubted that this was a factor in Jud trying to end his life. A young man in today's world didn't try to kill himself just because another man made a pass at him. She decided this was not a time to hold back. If she didn't ask, she thought, he would probably think she accepted his explanation. They would never get to the bottom of what really happened.

"I don't think you're telling me everything, Jud. I believe there's much more to this."

"I should have known you would figure that out, Dr. Goldman. I may be an inexperienced boy, as Dr. Bowen said; but I'm smart enough to know you wouldn't think that was a good enough reason to kill myself." His voice quivered with emotion. "He took everything away from me!" Tears welled up in his eyes. He flung himself out of the chair and walked to the window, his back to her.

"Take your time, Jud. I'm listening."

"It all began last semester when I was doing research on Shakespeare's *Henry V*. Most scholars seem to focus on the tragedies or the plays that are more ethereal, for example, *A Midsummer Night's Dream*. Personally, I have always been drawn the history plays. I've read and reread all of them, but my favorite is *Henry V*."

"I think it's one of my favorites too," Dr. Emily said. She nodded her head, encouraging him to continue.

"After extensive reading and study I was interested in how the play had been used as propaganda. Most people familiar with Shakespeare's history plays, especially *Henry V*, will immediately think of the famous Saint Crispin's Day speech:

We few, we happy few, we band of brothers.
For he today that sheds his blood with me
Shall be my brother; be he ne'er so vile,
This day shall gentle his condition.
And gentlemen in England now abed
Shall think themselves accursed they were not here,
And hold their manhoods cheap whiles any speaks
That fought with us upon Saint Crispin's Day.

Jud had turned from the window as he recited the famous lines. The sun was beginning to go down over the back garden, and the light from the window made a silhouette of his figure as he spoke the emotional words.

"I started thinking about how speeches like *Saint Crispin's Day* have been used to rally the troops all the way up to the present. Sir Laurence Olivier's *Henry V* was a patriotic movie filmed during the Second World War, a classic battle between good and evil. Then there's Kenneth Branagh's movie of *Henry V*, which seems to be emphasizing the horrors of war rather than glorifying it. By the way, his delivery of that speech is absolutely magnificent."

"I agree, Jud. Such violent scenes, but Branagh on horseback speaking those lines is unsurpassed. I can close my eyes and see him!"

Jud nodded in agreement. "But what really pushed me forward on the paper that was developing in my head was the discovery that The Royal National Theatre in London performed the play in 2003 with Henry as a modern general who was critical of the invasion of Iraq by the United States. I was really excited about how this was still a living play. I wanted to explore how it had been used as propaganda and reflect on how Shakespeare might have viewed its interpretation. I'm sure when he wrote the play the Hundred Years' War was still part of the public consciousness, and it would have been very unpopular to criticize Henry's invasion of France. The victory at the Battle of Agincourt would still be a source of national pride. Right?"

"Indeed. I have read various articles and reviews of the play, but can't think of a paper that looked at not only the use of the play as propaganda, but a comparison of the various interpretations. Excellent, Jud! I look forward to reading it."

"You're welcome to read it, of course, Dr. Emily. But I'm afraid Dr. Bowen beat me to it. It wasn't until second semester that I discovered that he had taken my research paper and published it. He used my idea and my research, changed a few words here and there, and the paper was accepted for publication in the *Journal of Shakespearian Studies!*"

Dr. Emily's face reflected her dismay. "I can't believe it! It's shocking to think that the head of our department would stoop so low as to steal a student's work. I despise academic dishonesty, although I'm not naive enough to think that it doesn't exist. From what I understand, at the larger universities it has become so prevalent that graduate students have taken safeguards to protect intellectual property. What is the world coming to?"

"I wish I had been smart enough to at least let someone else read the paper; perhaps I should have deposited a copy in the library, or put it on file in the department. Oh, it's too late now. The man is dead."

"I wonder . . ." Dr. Emily shook her head and appeared to be deep in thought. "Tell me how you found out about the article being published, Jud."

"He actually bragged about it, Dr. Emily! It must have been in February or early March. I went to the coffee shop in town for a break. He was there with a group of students, and I heard him talking about his latest publication. He saw me come in, and it almost seemed as if he wanted me to overhear. I went straight to the library and looked it up online. There it was; my paper, my research, in the *Journal of Shakespearian Studies* with his name, Dr. Basil Bowen as the author. I felt sick!"

"I can imagine you did. What did you do, Jud?"

"Confronted him of course! Again, he just made fun of me. Said there was nothing I could do. That I didn't have proof."

"Why didn't you come to me? I would have gone to the Dean. Merryvale prides itself in taking care of students and setting the highest standards." Dr. Emily's anger was growing.

"I had decided to do something, Dr. Emily. I kept going back and rereading the article. Did you know the Supreme Court of the United States had a mock trial for King Henry V to decide whether he was justified in invading France in 1415? Justices Samuel Alito and Ruth Bader Ginsburg presided and found that King Henry was justified in invading France. The section of the article that Dr. Bowen claimed to have written discussing the mock trial is taken directly from my paper, word for word, as is most of it."

"It is an outrage!" Dr. Emily was having difficulty controlling her emotions. Her sense of justice had been challenged. "For heaven's sake, Jud! You said you had made up your mind to speak up. What happened? How did things go so wrong that you gave up and tried to end your life?"

"That's what I'm getting around to, Dr. Emily. On the day I signed up for the part of the Clerk in the Faire, I decided to confront him one last time. I went to his office and told him I had made up my mind to report him to the Dean of the School of Arts and Sciences. I told him I wanted him to withdraw the paper and write an apology to the *Journal of Shakespearian Studies*. I didn't care what he said. He could claim there had been a mix-up in submitting the file for publication. I just wanted recognition for my work, and I wasn't going to let him take credit for it. I thought I was beginning to get through to him. He wasn't as arrogant as he had been on previous occasions."

"He obviously had very little to be arrogant about," Dr. Emily said softly, beginning to grasp the way things had happened that day in April.

"This is the part that is hardest to talk about. He made all kind of threats, but the one I really took seriously was that he would keep me from getting into any graduate school in the country. He said my academic career was over. He said he was tired of listening to my lies, and he would ruin my reputation. I was really frightened that he would keep me out of graduate school. It's been such a long struggle to get to where I am now, and I saw everything I had worked for dissolve with the look of sheer hate in that man's eyes."

"You believed he could do that? That was the reason you took the pills?"

"Yes, I just couldn't go on. I was terribly depressed and didn't know what to do. I don't have the kind of family you can turn to if you have a problem. Actually, I'm pretty much alone in the world. I didn't think it would matter to anyone."

"That's where you were wrong, Jud. It does matter. It matters to me and to more people than you can imagine."

Max chose this moment to wake from his nap. Sensing the tension in the room, his ears picked forward as he looked from one to the other and then without hesitation moved over and sat at Jud's feet, his sharp little eyes focused on the young man's face. Very slowly he positioned his head directly under Jud's hand so he could be petted.

"He never ceases to surprise me," said Dr. Emily. "Scotties are considered a one-person dog, you know. Oh, he tolerates Jess Thornton, but you're the first person I've ever seen him show the slightest bit of affection, besides myself, of course. It's a good omen, Jud. You've met with Maxwell of Dumfries's approval!"

Though so illustrious, he was very wise
And bore himself meekly as a maid.
He never yet had any vileness said,
In all his life, to whosoever wight.
He was a truly perfect, gentle knight.
****

THE KNIGHT
THE PROLOGUE TO THE CANTERBURY TALES
BY
GEOFFREY CHAUCER

Chapter 15

Jess Thornton's radio crackled to life, and his optimism about a peaceful day on the Merryvale campus immediately disappeared.   Here we go, he thought. "Thornton," he responded as he cruised across the brick paving in front of Main Hall.

The loud voice of the dispatcher cut through the dull pain he was feeling in his head. Pollen like a yellow mantle covered everything in sight. Azaleas, wisteria, and dogwood were all blooming in a riot of color on campus and on the manicured lawns of the town of Merryvale. It was Jess's favorite time of year; but like so many others, he suffered. Beauty sure does have its price, he thought. The radio in his car crackled to life, again.

"Sheriff Mitchell sends his regards and wants you to meet him at your regular place."

That new dispatcher had a voice that could wake the dead, he thought, or maybe it was just his headache making him overly sensitive to sound.

"Tell him I'll be there in five."

Jess suppressed a sneeze until he signed off. He bumped across the brick street and through the main gate of the campus toward downtown Merryvale and the local coffee house on Main Street. Kevin was already waiting in the almost empty parking lot as Jess pulled up beside him. Each officer ignored the parking spaces and positioned his car so the drivers' windows were next to each other, only a foot or so separating the vehicles.

Small towns made it necessary to take precautions, Jess reflected. He had learned through experience that the walls have ears in Merryvale. You would swear no one was around to overhear a conversation that was intended to be private and later discover that whatever was said was soon all over town. He thought about how many times he had seen patrol cars parked just like theirs with the officers talking to each other, arms resting at an angle through the open windows. In the past he had always assumed they were engaged in small talk, taking a break, maybe even goofing off. Now he knew otherwise. It was one sure way to not be overheard.

"What's up, Kev?" Jess managed to get out before the sneeze he had been suppressing so long cut him short.

"Man, I hope you're not contagious! Glad I decided to meet you out here in the open."

"Don't worry, just allergy. What's going on? Any news from the medical examiner? Seems like that report is taking forever. I know we were expecting it to take a while, but I heard the DA is anxious and is really putting on the pressure."

"Yeah, that's why I called you. Remember the Coroner's Office said it would take time to get the report back; and, considering the way the man died, they wanted to be careful. It doesn't look good, Jess. The toxicology report is back in, and it appears that our professor was poisoned."

"Damn. Just what we need. A murder investigation right here at the end of the semester with students and faculty ready to leave campus. You know most of them will want to go as soon as the graduation ceremony is over. At least the students will. I guess most of the faculty will be around for a few more days before taking their vacations."

"That's not really going to be a problem for the investigation, Jess. The district attorney has talked to Judge Franklin; and he's ordered that anyone closely associated with the case, students and faculty, must make themselves available for questioning. Not one person, even those who were simply bystanders and are witnesses to what took place that day at the Faire, can leave the county before they're interviewed by our office and make a statement."

"Good idea, but there'll be some unhappy folks."

"No doubt about that, but it can't be helped. We'll be handling the investigation, Jess; but we're depending on your support and assistance, just as we have in the past. We appreciate what the campus police force does for this community. It saves the Sheriff's Department a lot of patrol work having you here."

"Don't worry Kevin; my nose isn't out of joint. Actually, I'm glad you're in charge of this. I'm really too close to everyone involved to be objective about this case anyway."

"I'm glad you feel that way, Jess. I don't want you to think we're taking over your territory. And before I forget, I'm sure Dr. Goldman will be able to assist us. I would appreciate it if you would speak to her about helping us with her insights. After all, she's been a lot of help to us in the past."

"I'll talk to her right away and fill her in on the latest developments. It's going to be a shock for her when she finds out about Dr. Bowen."

"I guess everyone will be shocked except the person who did it. By the way, it would be best for me to not be seen with Dr. Emily too much during the investigation, just to play it safe. I don't want it to appear that we're relying on her in any way. It might tip off the killer, but since it's known that the two of you are friends I doubt anyone would notice if you seemed to be together more than usual. That way we would be playing it safe. We want to make certain Dr. Emily Goldman is well protected until we have the murderer in custody. "

Jess felt a cold shiver go up the back of his neck. The thought that Dr. Emily might be in danger if the killer found out she was assisting the police was something he hadn't thought about. He nodded to Kevin. "I'll talk with her this afternoon. It's hard to imagine a killer on the Merryvale campus. I don't like this at all, Kevin. It's hard to believe."

"I don't like it either. Just keep your eyes open, Jess. And be careful. It could be someone we least suspect. Once the killer finds out we know about the poison, the situation could get tricky." Kevin put his patrol car in reverse and started to back out of the parking lot.

"Wait!" Jess shouted.

Kevin eased the car back in place. Jess glanced around and lowered his voice as he made eye contact with Kevin through his open window. "You didn't say the kind of poison that was used. What was it? Maybe it was accidental, or is that wishful thinking?"

"I'm sorry to say that's wishful thinking, my friend. It was hemlock!"

"Hemlock! That's the last thing I would have thought of." Jess rubbed his nose with his handkerchief to ward off another sneeze.

"I must admit it surprised me too. I should have filled you in on what happened after Dr. Bowen arrived at the ER, Jess. I'm not thinking straight. I could use a good night's sleep. Anyway, I don't need to tell you that this is privileged information. We don't want anybody to know what type of poison was used. Dr. Emily will have to know of course, but we want to keep it quiet."

"Don't worry. I'll tell Dr. Emily. She knows that anything we tell her is strictly confidential."

"The ER physician on duty when they brought Dr. Bowen in was just a young guy, not too long out of completing his residency, I would imagine. Of course he did what he could. Ruled out a heart attack pretty quick. He thought it might be a stroke or something like that. It was the paralysis that led him in that direction, of a stroke, that is. He ventilated him, did everything possible; but the guy flat lined within a few minutes. There was no brain activity, no time to really make a diagnosis.

"They did blood work as soon as he arrived, I guess?" Jess was still trying to understand why and how anyone would give Dr. Bowen hemlock. Could it have been accidental or some sick joke?

"They did, the standard procedure, Jess. They drew blood; but before they could even look at it in the lab, he was dead. An autopsy was ordered, of course, tissue and blood samples sent off to be analyzed. Don't get me wrong; no one is faulting the hospital. If he had been at the Medical Center in Birmingham, I doubt they could have done anything. I've read up on it, and here's what I've found out. It can take anywhere from twenty minutes to three hours after the ingestion of hemlock for death to occur. If a person is treated quickly then the possibility for survival is good, but you have to know what you're dealing with. Well, that's all I can tell you for the time being. Stay in touch and go take some allergy medicine."

As Kevin drove away, Jess sat in his patrol car and tried to think of the best way to tell Dr. Emily that someone had murdered Dr. Basil Bowen and about the unusual cause of death. From now on their every encounter must seem casual and relaxed. It was way too early to try to make a guess, but it seemed possible that the murderer could be someone close to the English Department. He would have to take extra precautions. The last thing Jess wanted to do was to put Dr. Emily in danger by letting it be known that she was working with the police.

Somewhere on campus a murderer could possibly be watching their every move. Just to be on the safe side he would time his rounds through campus so he could give Dr. Emily a ride home that afternoon, something he had gotten into the habit of doing anyway since Jud's suicide attempt. She had seemed so vulnerable the afternoon he told her about Jud; there was fragility about her that he hadn't noticed before. Once he drove her home this afternoon, he would go in for one of their usual cups of tea and bring her up to date. Then he would be very careful not to been seen in public with her for several days, but someone on the campus police force would be watching her day and night. He would make sure of that.

Yea, die he shall, and in a shorter while
Than you require to walk but one short mile;
This poison is so violent and strong.
****
THE PARDONDER'S TALE
THE CANTERBURY TALES
BY
GOEFFREY CHAUCER

Chapter 16

"Hemlock!" Dr. Emily looked at Jess with eyes wide with surprise. "I must say I would never have imagined such a thing."

Dr. Emily put her tea cup down on the little mahogany table next to her chair. The late afternoon sun streamed through the double-hung window that looked out to her garden, casting a path of light across the jeweled tones of the Oriental rug on the study floor. Max, stretched out on his side, slept soundly, the sunlight turning his fur a bluish black. He was dreaming and his paws twitched as he chased something in his sleep. Dr. Emily sat gazing at the view for a moment as if she were a thousand miles away in thought. Slowly she turned her head toward her guest; her clear blue eyes looked steadily at him as she nodded her head. "But in a way it's appropriate."

Jess was still congratulating himself for arranging to casually happen along as Dr. Emily was walking across campus and offering her a ride home. To think that there was a murderer loose in Merryvale was shocking enough, but he was becoming more concerned than ever about keeping Dr. Emily out of harm's way. Now, as he took a sip of his tea, her words finally registered with him.

"Appropriate, Dr. Emily. What do you mean?"

"Well, it's so symbolic, isn't it?"

Jess looked at her blankly. "I'm sorry, Dr. Emily. I'm afraid you've lost me."

"Socrates, of course!" Her eyes sparkled.

"Yes, I admit that when I heard that it was hemlock I thought of Socrates. I guess most people associate it with him; but I'm sorry, I don't see anything symbolic about it."

"Socrates was condemned to death; and hemlock was his poison of choice, as you may remember; but what is significant in this case is that Socrates was convicted of corrupting the youth of Athens. Of course, that was the state's opinion. He was simply trying to encourage his students to question everything, something all corrupt governments find extremely dangerous, don't you think? So you could argue in a philosophical discussion that education, and thus the Socratic Method, is dangerous for the corrupt."

Jess was not certain where Dr. Emily was going with this, but long experience had taught him to hear her out.

"It was certainly dangerous for Dr. Bowen," she continued, "since someone was obviously questioning his methods of treating the youth and the faculty of this institution. Socrates, of course, had the education of his students as his purpose. I'm afraid the same cannot be said about Dr. Bowen. Yes, I think hemlock would be fitting, especially after what Jud revealed to me about Dr. Bowen's personality and his unpopularity with the student body." Dr. Emily paused for a moment before nodding her head in assent and continuing with her musings.

"That would certainly condemn him as a corrupter of the youth, not to mention academic dishonesty. Don't you agree, Jess?"

"I'm still not following you, Dr. Emily. Socrates drank the hemlock with the knowledge that he was taking his life—suicide. He felt honor-bound to save the state the trouble, but Dr. Bowen was murdered." Jess paused for a moment to think through another idea. "Or do you think it's possible that he drank hemlock in some symbolic gesture?"

"It makes you wonder, doesn't it? Was the hemlock chosen as a symbolic act or was it chosen for expediency? It is known to be a very fast-acting poison, you know. But put your mind at rest about one thing." She turned and looked squarely at Jess. "No, indeed, I believe without a shadow of a doubt that it was not suicide. Dr. Bowen was much too convinced of his own importance to ever consider taking his own life. But it was symbolic, Jess. It was an execution and there was a message behind it!"

Jess looked at Dr. Emily with amazement. How could she possibly know so much about the case already? The police had only just opened the murder investigation; the coroner had ruled that a murder had been committed by a person or persons unknown, and already Dr. Emily seemed to know much more about the motives behind the crime than the police could ever hope to understand.

No wonder Jess's mind was in a whirl. Not only was he worried about Dr. Emily, he was also concerned about keeping the details of the case a secret. It would be difficult getting through the last few weeks of classes without the real cause of Dr. Bowen's death slipping out, especially in a small town like Merryvale where gossip was rampant, Jess thought. For the present, the college community assumed that poor Dr. Bowen had dropped dead of a heart attack or some other physical infirmity. Before long, however, everyone in town would know about the poison. So how was Dr. Emily already aware of something more sinister, Jess wondered. He and Kevin had gone over every possible scenario, trying to piece the motives and possible suspects together. He studied Dr. Emily's cherubic face intently. What went on in that mind of hers, he wondered.

"I'm sorry, Jess, for not being totally honest with you; but I see now that there's no way that I can possibly remain silent about what I know about Dr. Bowen and the possible implications. You must promise me that you'll think carefully about what I have to tell you. I want the person responsible for this crime to be the only one to answer for it, and I'm afraid that there is more than one person with reasons enough to be the executioner and administer the hemlock. At the same time it's possible that lives may be ruined or, at the very least, reputations damaged if we are not very cautious and make certain the information we have is not allowed to go beyond the walls of this room. Of course, Sheriff Mitchell must be told, but no one else. You know what this little town is like."

"I promise, Dr. Emily. I know you understand that I

can't withhold information that may be relevant to a murder investigation, but I will always be guided by you and share your thoughts on a need-to-know-only basis.

"Then we understand each other, Jess, as always. Now, I regret that I must tell you a sad story about a young man who was abused. It was told to me in the strictest confidence; but now that Dr. Bowen is dead, the truth must come out, no matter how it might reflect on the college."

Dr. Emily told Jess everything about Dr. Bowen's treatment of Jud: the sexual advances, the theft of Jud's work, the attempt at blackmail, and the enormity of the betrayal that resulted in Jud's attempt at suicide.

Jess could barely contain his outrage. "What a fool! How did he think he could get away with that kind of behavior? I must admit I didn't care for the man. No, that is an understatement. I thought he was an arrogant bastard. I'm sorry, Dr. Emily. I apologize for the language, but he must have thought he could do anything he pleased and never be caught."

"I'm sure that's exactly the way he thought. But that's where he was wrong," Dr. Emily mused. "He made the mistake of thinking he was smarter than everyone else. He was constantly referring to his degree from Oxford, as if that made him far superior to the rest of us. It would be interesting to investigate his record there and see if we can gain any insights from his years of study at that institution.

Jess nodded. "I'm sure Sheriff Mitchell will conduct an investigation of Bowen's background. With the information you've just given me, we will get to the bottom of this. A good place to start and the easiest to check would be with the dean at his former institution in Virginia. I'm sure he came here with highest recommendations, but it won't hurt to check out what they thought of him there. It might take more time to check on the Oxford connection, but we'll get that as well."

"I'm sure he did have an excellent recommendation, but I wouldn't put much value on praise from a former employer. That is one sure way of getting rid of someone you no longer want to employ with as little fuss as possible."

"You shock me, Dr. Emily!" Jess replied. "Are you telling me that the academic community is just as bad as the corporate world?"

"I'm afraid so, Jess. Unfortunately, human nature is not improved by advanced degrees. You've seen several examples of that on our own little campus in the past."

"Yes, unfortunately, I'll have to agree with you. I'll pass along the word to Sheriff Mitchell that we should start looking into Dr. Bowen's life in Virginia and then see what we can find out from Oxford University."

"An excellent plan." Dr. Emily nodded her head in approval and took another sip of her tea.

"A word of caution before I leave you, Dr. Emily. The press will probably arrive in droves once they hear about the murder ruling. At this point most people still think it was a heart attack or a stroke, but eventually it will leak out that poison was the cause of death. We must be very careful to not release the type of poison that killed Dr. Bowen. The longer we can keep that a secret the more we'll be able to find out from the people we'll be interviewing. There'll have to be some sort of explanation, of course; but we need to be careful and not give anything away. Just be careful what you say, Dr. Emily. In all likelihood someone closely connected to the college, maybe even someone in the English Department, is a killer."

"I'm sure half the town already knows about the hemlock, Jess. You know Merryvale, and don't worry. I'll be careful."

O Cupido, that know'st not charity!
O Despot, that no peer will have with thee!
Truly it is said, that love, like all lordship,
Declines, with little thanks, a partnership.
****
THE KNIGHT'S TALE
THE CANTERBURY TALES
BY
GEOFFREY CHAUCER

Chapter 17

After he left Dr. Emily's house, Jess decided to call Glenda and see whether she had plans for dinner. It had been a while since he had been able to spend any time with her, but he hesitated for a moment. The relationship had gone a bit faster than Jess would have preferred; but he was a very attractive, single man; and there was no reason why he shouldn't enjoy the company of any of the ladies of legal age on campus that struck his fancy.

Of course with a murder investigation in progress, he wasn't sure if socializing with anyone in the English Department was such a good idea. He struggled with his conscience for a moment and then thought; what the hell; they had to eat. He grabbed his cell phone and dialed her number.

"Of course," Glenda purred, "I'll be delighted to see you. I'll fix something for dinner if you're hungry."

"Dinner sounds great. Actually, I'm starved."

No sooner had the call ended than Jess began to worry all over again if this was really a wise idea. Technically, everyone in the English Department who had close contact with Dr. Bowen could be considered a suspect, but Glenda was only the administrative assistant; and as far as he knew, there was nothing that could connect her to the murder. He tried to rationalize his desire to be with Glenda and his obligation to duty as a police officer. Campus police did not carry the same sort of prestige, at least in the opinion of the public, that regular police officers enjoyed; but his military training made him sensitive to protocol. Besides, the campus police were technically not involved in the investigation of the murder of Dr. Bowen, he rationalized. The case was being handled by the county law enforcement agencies, after all; so there was really no conflict of interest.

He soothed his conscience by telling himself that he was more than aware of his responsibilities as a professional, and he was happy to let the Sheriff's

Department handle the investigation. His duties had been described to him as keeping his "ear to the ground" on campus. Just how was he supposed to do that, he wondered if he wasn't making his rounds and chatting with those who crossed his path? There was no way he was going to know what was being talked about or how the students and faculty felt about the tragedy if he isolated himself from everyone in the department, he convinced himself.

Actually, he was certain Glenda could be a great help in the investigation. She was one of the more talkative members of the English Department and her position as office administrator put her in the position to know more about the business of the department than almost anyone else. Jess felt she would be able to share insights on the case. Still, he didn't want to be accused of socializing with the staff. He began to think they should probably see less of each other, but he was confident that once the investigation was over and the murderer was apprehended all would return to normal.

After his duties were over that afternoon, he returned to his apartment, showered and shaved, and presented himself at Glenda's cottage door determined to discuss the awkward position he was in. He hoped he would be able to explain things to her without upsetting her too much.

Surely she knew that he enjoyed her company enormously and wouldn't take it personally if his visits were scarce or even nonexistent while the investigation was under way. Jess had gotten the impression that Glenda was a highly emotional woman. He wanted to avoid a scene and tears, although he wasn't certain that Glenda's feelings for him were serious. Determined to have a pleasant evening, he rang the doorbell. The chime played the first few bars of *Song of Joy*. Jess tried, without much success, to suppress a laugh.

Within seconds Glenda flung the door open and smothered him in an embrace; her well-developed breasts rubbed against his chest. She stood on tiptoe and kissed him on the cheek followed by a much longer kiss on the mouth. Jess steered her into the foyer and quickly pulled the door shut behind him, always conscious of the prying eyes of the neighbors.

"Come right in, you big handsome man! I was afraid I was going to have to spend the evening alone, and I must admit, the idea of doing that was rather depressing. Especially after hearing the dreadful news that Dr. Bowen was murdered! I must admit I feel a little uneasy here by myself.

"News travels fast. When did you find out about it?"

"Kevin Mitchell came by the office this afternoon. He wanted the names and addresses of all of the English

Department faculty and the students who are English majors or work part time in the department. He kept asking me so many questions. I felt like I was being interrogated as well, Jess!"

"Well, he's just following the proper procedure. You mustn't take it personally, Glenda. I guess he told you that in a murder investigation everyone who had any connection with the deceased has to be questioned?"

"I didn't have my wits about me, after the shock of hearing such dreadful news, to ask Sheriff Mitchell what killed him. I know he was sick the morning of the Faire, a stomach virus, he said. He was riding at the head of the procession, and then he was suddenly stricken down. Kevin Mitchell said Dr. Bowen had been poisoned! How could that have happened, Jess? This seems like such a sleepy little backwater of a place. That's one of the reasons I wanted to move here. You know, get away from the rat race and crime."

"It normally is a very peaceful place, Glenda."

"I don't know how we're going to get through the next few weeks with exams and graduation. Do you realize we only have two weeks left in the semester?"

"Did he tell you no one closely associated with the English Department is allowed to leave the area until the police have had the opportunity to interview them and make a statement?"

"Why don't you just go ahead and say suspects, Jess? I guess we're all under suspicion until the case is closed, aren't we?"

"I'm afraid that's true, Glenda, which does bring up a slight problem I need to talk to you about. I'm not taking part in the investigation in any official capacity, but I'm working here on campus assisting the Sheriff's Department. I need to be very careful about socializing with anyone who's being questioned by the police. From a professional standpoint it just wouldn't look good. I hope you understand. I came by to tell you in person. I'm sorry about dinner, but maybe we should wait until all of this is over. It's not that I don't want to see you; in fact, there's nothing I would like better."

"But that's ridiculous! Jess, how could you think I would be involved in a murder?"

"I don't think that, Glenda. I'm just trying to explain to you why I think it would be a good idea to not socialize with each other until the murderer is caught."

"Well, I suppose from a professional standpoint I can understand, and I won't take it personally; but since you're here you might as well stay and have dinner with me. I know; we'll eat out in the garden and have a glass of wine, maybe two, and then we'll see what I can talk you into. It's such a beautiful evening, especially to have dinner under the stars. If this is my last opportunity to be alone with you for a while, I want to make the most of it."

"I came over with the best of intentions, but it appears I'm morally weak. Lead on to the garden. Isn't that where Adam met his downfall?"

"I believe it was, my dear. Come on. I'll give you a tour!"

The next morning as Jess made his way back to his apartment, he felt like an adolescent slipping in after his curfew. It was a feeling he had no intention of repeating. No matter how tempting it might be to enjoy Glenda's company, he would not let it happen again until the case was closed. After checking his voice mail, he put in a call to Kevin and set up a meeting. He wanted to fill him in on what Dr. Emily had told him about Jud Sharpe's suicide attempt and the academic theft allegedly committed by Dr. Bowen.

The beauty of the late spring morning seemed to pale as Jess thought about the nature of the evil that must have possessed Basil Bowen. A person in a position of trust, working with young people, should never be allowed to have the power to destroy lives. Unfortunately, it would appear that he had almost destroyed Jud. No wonder someone felt so strongly about Dr. Bowen's actions that he could view murder as justifiable. But who could have possibly hated him so much? It could have been a number of people, he supposed, either here on campus or someone from his past life. Jess cringed at the thought that it could be someone from Merryvale; and although he didn't want to think about it, he realized Jud would be under suspicion when the facts were known. He could understand revenge, but taking another life was so risky. Why not just report him to the authorities? Then Dr. Emily's words came back to him, and he remembered what she had told him the previous afternoon.

She had asked Jud the same question. "No one would take my word against his," Jud had said. A sick feeling rose in the pit of Jess's stomach. Surely it wasn't the boy.

At county sessions was he lord an sire,
And often acted as a knight of shire.
A dagger and a trinket-bag of silk
Hung from his girdle, white as morning milk.
He had been sheriff and been auditor;
And nowhere was a worthier vavasor.
****

THE FRANKLIN
THE PROLOGUE OF THE CANTERBURY TALES
BY
GEOFFREY CHAUCER

Chapter 18

Kevin Mitchell sat at his desk in the Sinclair County Sheriff's Office sunk in a dark mood. Every murder investigation he had taken part in since he had been in law enforcement had a limited number of suspects. Usually, a close family member or associate would prove to be the guilty party. He or she would be arrested and indicted when the prosecution felt there was enough evidence for a conviction.

The murder of Dr. Basil Bowen involved way too many variables to suit Kevin Mitchell. There were just too many people at Merryvale College who had a motive and were on his suspect list. He thought there could very possibly be others in the town or from the college in Virginia who would be more than happy to see Basil Bowen no longer among the living, unknown suspects.

Two days had crept slowly by since the toxicology report of poisoning by hemlock had been verified, and the coroner had ruled the death a homicide by person or persons unknown. Time was now a critical factor, with the end of the spring semester and graduation fast approaching. The district attorney was leaning on Kevin pretty hard to present some concrete evidence as soon as possible. During the last two days, the investigation had slowly gotten underway, but Kevin was seeing very little progress in solving the case. In other words, the investigation was going nowhere, and without any physical evidence he was not looking forward to his next meeting with the district attorney.

After all, too much time had passed and Mother Nature had been at work; how could there possibly be any sort of physical evidence just lying around on the grounds of the college? It seemed futile for forensics to go over the route the pilgrims had taken across campus in search of any shred of evidence that could be tied to the murder. There had been several spring showers since the Faire, and no telling how many students had walked along the brick streets and across the lawns since then. Hell, the groundskeepers had probably mowed the grass at least once, maybe twice, since then, Kevin thought. But an effort was made just in case; even the campus stable had been examined inch by inch. It was no surprise that this time consuming search had found absolutely nothing. In the meantime, the slow process of checking the background of Dr. Bowen was underway, and the Oxford connection would have to be checked out as well.

Kevin's first inquiry had been to the dean of Dr. Bowen's college in Virginia. Before he made the call, he had obtained a copy of the letter of recommendation sent to the office of the Dean of the College of Arts and Sciences at Merryvale when Dr. Bowen had applied for the job over a year before. He had read the letter aloud to the dean during their first phone conversation, just in case his memory needed to be refreshed.

"Dean Watson, is there anything you can tell me about Dr. Bowen that's not mentioned in this glowing letter of recommendation?" Kevin inquired. "Did he make any enemies while he was at your institution? Did he get along well with others in the department?" The questions and answers during their phone conversation were being recorded with the dean's permission; but when things got a little too personal and the questions continued, the dean requested that he be allowed to consult with the attorney the college kept on retainer. It was Kevin's opinion that his questions about how well Dr. Bowen got along with his wife, Elise, and if there had been any indication that he was perhaps unfaithful, involved with another woman, seemed to be what set off the alarm.

Looks like he'll have to be subpoenaed, Kevin thought gloomily as he pushed papers around on his desk. He was expecting a visit from Jess Thornton and wished he would hurry up, so they could go over some of the things that were bothering him. He understood Jess had to get someone to cover for him at the college, but he was anxious to talk to him again about the list of possible suspects and get his recommendations on the interview process. Kevin's impatience was growing. Jess knew most of these people fairly well and saw them on a daily basis. His insights would very likely shed some light on the investigation, and Kevin was fretting over the lack of progress in the case.

There was a sharp rap at his office door. Jess walked in, took one look at Kevin, and knew his friend was feeling the heat. "What can I do to help, Kevin?"

"I've got a list somewhere on this desk—just a minute. There's fresh coffee if you want it"

"Thanks, coffee might help. I can't remember when I had a good night's sleep."

"Me either. Good, here's the list. First, I talked to the dean in Virginia. I thought he was going to give up some information, but I think he got nervous. He wants to consult the college attorney. That's never a good sign. I suspect that letter of recommendation was written to get rid of Dr. Basil Bowen. I believe you told me that Dr. Goldman had suggested that might be the case. They write a letter praising the guy like he came down on a silver cloud, and it turns out he's really a jerk! That way they get rid of him and send him on to be a problem somewhere else. Dr. Goldman might very well be right about that. That was just a feeling I got talking to the dean, nothing really specific."

"That's what Dr. Goldman suggested." Jess nodded. "She said the academic world is no less corrupt than the corporate world. Those weren't her exact words, but that's what she meant."

"She's a smart woman, no doubt about that. By the way, I'm going to start calling people in to ask routine questions: where they were before the riders mounted up on the morning of the Faire, what they thought about Dr. Bowen, how well they knew him. You know the routine. Here's the list of people I have so far. I would appreciate it if you and Dr. Goldman would go over it, and see whether there're any additional insights you could give me on the personality of these people.

Dr. Goldman is in almost daily contact with most of them, and I trust her judgment. You know, Jess, she has the uncanny quality of appearing to inhabit another world from the rest of us; but you and I know better, don't we? As a result people rarely keep their guard up around her. They think she's just another academic lost in the Middle Ages, thinking about Geoffrey Chaucer or some obscure Anglo Saxon manuscript. You agree?"

"Yep. Nothing about people's behavior seems to shock Dr. Emily. She's not locked up in an ivory tower. I'm sure she knows how cruel the world can be. She's nobody's fool. Give me the list and we'll go over it together. I think she has a three-hour seminar this afternoon, so I'll pick her up at Tutwiler Hall and drive her home. I've been making a habit of doing that. She had the foresight to mention to several people that the walk home is beginning to get to be a little too much for her. Not true, of course, but we didn't want people to think we're working together on police business. This gives me more opportunities to talk to her without it appearing that we're up to something. She will be much more effective if everyone continues to think she has her head in the clouds."

Kevin shifted restlessly in his chair. "Now that you've had time to think about the case, Jess, who's at the top of your list?"

"The most obvious would be the wife, I suppose. That's who I thought of right away, especially since she's made no secret of the fact that she's a very unhappy woman. It could have been a domestic thing that had been brewing for a long time. Don't forget they had a very public argument on the day of the Faire, before everyone mounted up. By the way, Dr. Bowen looked like a pretty sick man during that little scene if I remember correctly. She could have given him the poison before they left home."

"If that's a possibility we need to get a search warrant for their house. There might be evidence there, but she's probably too smart to leave anything incriminating lying around. Don't you think? Anyway, with the time factor, she could've easily gotten rid of it." Kevin said.

Jess stopped to collect his thoughts, took a sip of coffee, and nodded in agreement. "But there are other possibilities that have to be considered. Dr. Bowen, as it turns out, has not exactly endeared himself to many people at the college. There's no need for me to explain the culture of this small Southern town to you. Hospitality and graciousness are still a way of life here. You know what I mean—you grew up here like I did. I think most people were willing to give them a little time and thought that, even if they got off to a rocky start, they would settle in and be a great addition to the community. In other words, I don't think there was any resentment associated with him being an outsider at the beginning. But it didn't take him long to upset most of the professors in the department, and his wife let it be known that she thought she was too good to be here. All that talk about her illustrious ancestors in whatever county she's from in Virginia didn't exactly endear her to the natives."

"Spotsylvania County, I believe," Kevin replied. "She's supposed to be descended from early settlers. Virginia bluebloods, according to her, who lost all their money during the Civil War. Same old story all the 'Want-a-be' Southern Belles tell. She trapped me at one of the parties I attended over the Christmas holidays. Wasn't going to give me the time of day until she found out I'm about to finish law school. I guess that made my stock go up in her book. Anyway, she struck me as a phony."

Kevin turned on his printer and made a copy of the list of people he planned to interview and handed it to Jess. "Let me know what you and Dr. Goldman think about this list. Not everyone whose name is on it is a suspect from my point of view, but they may have been in a position to see or hear something that will help with the investigation."

Jess looked over the names. There were no surprises. Even Rich Henry would be interviewed, although it would be hard to imagine what kind of motive he would have had to murder Dr. Bowen. Jess seemed to remember that Rich thought Dr. Bowen was a good horseman, high praise in Rich's book. If the victim had been Elise Bowen, it would have been an entirely different matter. The sidesaddle incident was still being discussed and laughed about on campus.

"I see Jud Sharp's name is on the list, Kevin. I don't know how Dr. Goldman will take that. You know he's her protégé."

"I thought about that, but I think Dr. Goldman can handle just about anything, Jess."

"I suppose so, but I'd like to spare her as much as I can. If Jud Sharp is involved in this in any way, it'll be devastating for her. She's never married, you know. No children of her own. All of her hopes are on Jud and his academic career. You know how people say we relive our lives through our children. Well, I don't know about that since I'm not married; but I would think that Dr. Goldman sees her legacy continuing with Jud, her academic legacy, that is. After all, teaching has been her life's purpose."

Now is not that of God a full great grace
That such a lewed mann's wit shall pass
The wisdom of a heap of learned men.
****

THE MANCIPLE
THE PROLOGUE OF THE CANTERBURY TALES
BY
GEOFFREY CHAUCER

Chapter 19

"I put very little faith in written letters of recommendation, Jess. I think we discussed this earlier. Dr. Emily settled into one of the Adirondack chairs grouped around a small table in her garden. People are very hesitant to put negative comments about people down on paper—afraid of libel and lawsuits would be my guess. Looking back, I suppose that not enough time was taken to thoroughly investigate Dr. Bowen's background before he came to us. Everyone was in too much of a hurry. They were afraid I would accept the position!" Dr. Emily laughed. "But that is neither here nor there. The man is dead. Our problem is to try to find out who poisoned him and who would have the desire to do it in such a public manner. It's as if the murderer wanted as many people as possible to see him see him suffer. Revenge must have played a great part in the mind of the murderer, don't you think?"

"No doubt it did, Dr. Emily. It was premeditated, not spur of the moment. Such a gruesome death and for it to take place in public made it much more dramatic and shocking. But let's not think too much about Dr. Bowen's final moments right now. Personally I wish the man had died at home in his bed; but, unfortunately, we have a very complicated murder scene. Let's just put our heads together and see what we can come up with. Sheriff Mitchell has given us a list of people he will be interviewing, and he is interested in hearing your insights."

The evening was pleasant in Dr. Emily's garden. The unpredictability of spring had finally given way to the warmth of May, and the flowers in the garden were flourishing before the heat of summer set in. As much as Dr. Emily loved flowers, she left the selection and planting to a local man who had taken care of the lawn and landscaping for many years. The academic life left her little time for the physical labor required to maintain a pleasant outdoor area to entertain.

Max was thoroughly enjoying his evening outside with human company. He made certain that they noticed that he was defending the garden from all intruding birds and other flying creatures. Occasionally he would give a short bark if he saw someone passing on the street. He made his rounds, smelling everything as he went. Finally he settled down next to Dr. Emily's chair. Her hand caressed the top of his head as he finally stretched out for one of his short naps.

"Did you know that my father was a botanist, Jess? Oh, not by profession. He was a lawyer in Chicago, but it was one of his passions. He taught me a great deal about the world of plants during those long snowy winters. I miss working in my garden and planning what flowers to select each year, but my time is absorbed these days with my studies and my students. I simply don't have the time. Perhaps one day when I retire I'll get involved in gardening again. It's so therapeutic."

"Your gardener does an excellent job, but I'm sure you must make some suggestions. You amaze me with your knowledge of so many things: art, music, literature, and now I find you're interested in botany, as well."

"I'm a mere amateur, Jess, only an amateur."

She had suggested that they sit outside for a while before the sun went down. She knew one of the people on the list Kevin had sent over was bound to be Jud, and she could still see him in her mind's eye pacing the floor of her study as he told her about how he had been treated by Dr. Bowen. Somehow she couldn't stand the idea of talking about him in that room.

"I know who you're most concerned about, Dr. Emily," Jess said softly. "I'm sure you know Jud is on the list to be questioned since he is a student assistant in the English Department and took a class with Dr. Bowen."

"I suppose my thoughts are rather transparent these days. Yes, I will admit my main concern has been with Jud since the beginning."

"You don't suppose he had anything to do with it, do you?"

"No! Of course not! But when and if facts are known about the reason for his attempt at suicide, I'm afraid he will be placed under suspicion."

"You know I haven't talked to Kevin about Jud's conflict with Dr. Bowen. I probably should have told him, but today was the first opportunity I've had to see the list of people he plans to question. I decided to keep quiet about it. I thought it would be best for Jud to come forward and tell Kevin the truth about what really happened. It will look better for the boy if he presents the facts to the Sheriff, rather than having him hear it through the grapevine. Actually, I was rather relieved that Kevin didn't ask me too many questions about the people on the list, just handed it over; but I'm sure he'll get around to it eventually. Kevin will be a good, perhaps a great, lawyer, you know. He doesn't want to let anything influence him. He's a fair and impartial officer."

"Yes, I believe you're right about his character. I have confidence he will do the right thing as he sees it. It's just that Jud does seem to be one of the people to have a motive for the murder, a powerful motive. Don't misinterpret that remark. I'm certain he had no part in it, but I told him to tell Sheriff Mitchell everything he told me—all the sordid details! "

"Good. I'm glad you gave him that advice, even though it won't be easy. Let's hope he tells Kevin the whole story. It will look better for Jud to be up front about the whole thing. There're probably several other people who would have a reason to want to see Dr. Bowen dead. Some we might not even know about yet. The man seems to have made a lot of enemies, Dr. Emily. Don't worry too much. I don't think Jud is the only one with a motive."

Dr. Emily looked thoughtful. "I'm sure Elise Bowen will be one of the first persons the police will consider very carefully. In most cases, I believe, a family member is usually at the top of the list of suspects, especially if there seems to be a problem in their relationship. An unhappy spouse is always considered before anyone else, I suppose. It's unfortunate that so many people heard the argument Elise and Basil had as everyone was preparing to mount up at the stable. The police won't have to look far for a witness to that drama."

Jess nodded. "She has a loud voice; that's for sure. More than a few people heard her last words to her husband: 'I hate you, Basil!' It will be hard for most folks to forget that."

"Do you think she will be the prime suspect, Jess? I'm sure she will be in most people's minds, but I'm not so sure I would put her at the top of the list. If a woman is smart, and I'm not suggesting she is, but let's say she's of average intelligence and that she planned to poison him, the last thing she would want to do would be to make a statement like that in public and create a scene. Of course, she does have a tendency to be rather high strung and lose her temper. She may have let her emotions get in the way of her judgment. If she did poison him, her public display that morning was a serious mistake."

Jess, who had been standing up during their conversation, nervously pacing back and forth in front of Dr. Emily, finally flung himself down in a chair and nodded in agreement. "She could have done it. She had a history of speaking abusively to him. I observed that on the night I went over to question him about Jud's suicide attempt. She was very unpleasant. But in all fairness he wasn't exactly prince charming either. He showed no sympathy for Jud, no concern for a student in his department who had almost lost his life. It seemed to be all about him, trying to absolve himself of any responsibility. You can imagine the way the conversation went, I'm sure. They both seemed so unfeeling. Their whole attitude put me off. I'm not sure I'm capable of being objective about the man, but I don't suppose I'll be alone feeling that way."

"No indeed. I'm afraid he made enemies here from the beginning. So where does this leave us, Jess? We know it wasn't Jud, or at least I'm certain that he didn't do it. Elise is a strong possibility as an unhappy spouse. Who else is under suspicion?"

"Who knows, quite a few I would imagine. The killer could be someone from his old school in Virginia. Have you thought of that? There was a big crowd this year for the Faire, larger than usual, I believe. Some unknown person who held a grudge against Dr. Bowen could have been there and no one would have ever known. The Faire is well publicized and would be an excellent opportunity for someone to blend into the crowd. Lots of people were in costume and heavy makeup, the perfect chance for a person to conceal his identity. It would have been possible for anyone to have given him a drink containing the hemlock, and he was seen by a large number of people drinking out of a flask. But let's not get off track with that right now. We need to think about what we know for sure."

"Who else would have a motive?" Dr. Emily paused a moment to collect her thoughts. "He had ruffled a lot of feathers. As far as faculty members are concerned, Dr. Aquilla Greer was angry about having his courses changed. He viewed that as an insult to the years he has devoted to research and his expertise in his field. Then there is Dr. Melanie Adams. Dr. Bowen publically humiliated her by announcing at an English Department open house with many visitors in attendance that American Literature was inferior, a waste of instructional time, I believe he said."

"He was a real jerk, wasn't he?" Jess felt his anger rise. "He must have thought he was so superior to everyone else. I suppose Dr. Greer and Dr. Adams could have held a grudge, but was it enough to poison him?"

"I have to agree with your observation about his personality, but those two could not possibly be seriously considered as suspects, Jess. I've known Dr. Greer for years, and Dr. Adams is one of the meekest women I've ever met, such a sweet person. She was crushed and embarrassed by his comments, of course, but the idea of her retaliating in any way is unthinkable. I'm positive neither of them would ever think of harming anyone. Yes, they were both hurt and humiliated. But they would never take someone's life!"

"I tend to agree. You do know that Sheriff Mitchell plans on calling you in for questioning as well, don't you?" This was the moment he had been uncertain about. He was afraid Dr. Emily would be greatly offended.

"Well, of course. He will have to, won't he? It would seem very peculiar to most people if everyone in the department is called in and questioned and I'm skipped over. I'm not offended in the least, Jess. There must be a thorough investigation."

"I'm relieved you feel that way, Dr. Emily."

"The crucial issue is that we're missing too many pieces to the puzzle. I'm anxious to hear from Oxford University and discover what light they can shed on the time Basil Bowen spent with them. And I hope Dean Watson in Virginia will be forthcoming with information. At the moment, that's what's keeping me up at night. I hope that whoever murdered him is not one of our own, Jess. That would be very hard to live with."

"That's what I'm hoping for too, but I'm afraid we're not going to find any easy answers. This investigation is shaping up to be a long one. Kevin said he may have to make a quick trip up to Virginia and nose around. They're being very tight-lipped about our deceased professor at his former college. One thing I do know is that arrangements have been made with the administration for the Sheriff's Department to use one of the conference rooms in Tutwiler Hall to do the preliminary questioning of those on the list. There were some objections from some of the faculty, and I can see their point of view. They thought police business shouldn't be brought onto the campus, but it makes sense. It will be much more convenient since those being interviewed are closely associated with the college, and the Sheriff's office is on the other side of the county. Students without transportation and those unable to drive over for questioning would have to be shuttled back and forth. It would be time-consuming and take a lot of manpower."

"I'm not quite sure how I feel about that, Jess. It will no doubt speed up the process, especially since we're so close to the end of the semester and graduation. But conducting the questioning here will cast a shadow on what should be a happy time for our graduates, especially for Jud Sharp." Dr. Emily looked wistfully around the garden. "Do you suppose we'll ever get our peaceful little campus back?"

"I'm afraid it depends on how quickly we're able to find the murderer."

Jess's cell phone gave three sharp rings. "Thornton, here," he answered.

Jess turned to Dr. Emily and briefly made eye contact. She knew without having to speak that he needed a private moment and nodded for him to go. She noticed the tension in his body as he walked away from her across the garden and then stopped as if struck by a thunderbolt. He nodded his head, as if in agreement, and continued to talk softly as he paced along the path that crossed the lawn to the iron fence nearest the street. Although his voice was muted, she was certain she heard an exclamation of surprise. Something has happened she thought! Some new information has been discovered. Dr. Emily had an uncanny knack for reading body language and tone of voice. She suddenly felt a surge of excitement herself. Instinctively, she knew that the investigation was about to move forward.

Jess punched the button on his cell phone, ending the call, turned, and gave her a penetrating look. Slowly he walked toward her and sat down again. Damn these chairs, he thought. They were designed to look stylish, he guessed, but were not very comfortable for the kind of extended discussion he knew was coming.

"Let's go inside, Dr. Emily. We don't want to run the risk of being overheard. That was Sheriff Mitchell with information from England." He got up stiffly and took her arm as they walked quickly into the house. Max trotted along behind them, his short legs hurrying to keep up. Once they were inside, Jess made a quick tour around the house making sure the front door was locked and that all was secure before they settled in the study. Max trailed along behind him, on patrol and alert. He sensed something in the air; the tension and anxiety were palpable, and he wasn't about to let anything get past him. He emitted a few low growls deep in his throat as only a Scottie can do.

"For goodness sake, Jess! What's happened? Even Max knows something is going on."

"Sheriff Mitchell got a call from England just a short time ago. It seems it took the officials at Oxford more time than expected to respond to the department's inquiry. There was some confusion there about the academic records, so they called in their local law enforcement officers. Now the Oxford Police have been called into the investigation. They suspect that there's been some tampering done and a security breach, but the major revelation is that our man, Dr. Basil Bowen, is a fraud. The real Dr. Basil Bowen, a graduate of Oxford University, died three years ago in a diving accident while on vacation in Corsica!"

Dr. Emily looked thunderstruck. "But who on earth was this man who had us so convinced he was a legitimate graduate of that noble institution, and how did he make fools of us all?"

"I'm afraid we have no idea, no idea at all."

"You mean the authorities in England have no idea either? How shocking!"

"No, so far they haven't been able to identify him, but the situation is being taken very seriously. Oxford will most likely be calling in Scotland Yard. I wish I had more to tell you, and I'm afraid I have to leave you now, Dr. Emily. Sherriff Mitchell and I need to go over what little we do know and make plans. I'm afraid he'll have no choice but to go up to Virginia in the morning and interview Dean Watson."

Jess ran his fingers through his hair and briefly massaged his forehead. "Not only do we have a murderer on our hands, but a serious case of identity theft and academic fraud as well. This puts an entirely new perspective on the case. Keep your doors locked, Dr. Emily, and don't hesitate to call the emergency number if you feel uneasy about anything. One of the campus officers could be here in just a few minutes."

"I'll be careful, Jess, but I don't imagine anyone would try to harm me. Besides, Max will sound the alarm if someone tries to get in."

"To be truthful, I'm not sure of anything at this point or what we're dealing with. The closer we get to the bottom of this the more desperate the murderer may become. If he thinks we know his identity, there's no telling what he might do. We can't trust anybody at this point. Just be careful, Dr. Emily."

As hot he was, and lecherous, as a sparrow
****
THE SUMMONER
THE PROLOGUE OF THE CANTERBURY TALES
BY
GEOFFREY CHAUCER

Chapter 20

"Thanks for picking me up, Jess. It was a hell of a trip." Kevin Mitchell's whole demeanor showed the fatigue of the last twenty-four hours. As the lights of the Birmingham Airport faded from view, Jess's car cruised up the entrance ramp to the interstate heading southwest toward Merryvale. Jess pressed down on the accelerator until he was doing the speed limit and slowly the lights of town were only a faint glow in the rearview mirror.

"Birmingham to Atlanta to D.C. Then the drive over to Virginia and back again. I'm not sure I'll be making good sense, Jess; but this is just as good a time as any to talk privately. Anything I forget to tell you can be filled in tomorrow."

"I'm listening, Kevin."

"Dean Watson was not exactly thrilled to see me. I just showed up at his office. You know, Jess, from the beginning, since you and Dr. Goldman put it in my mind that they might be glad to see Dr. Bowen go, I've wondered about the integrity of anyone who would write a recommendation for someone they didn't like or trust. Oh well, enough about that for now. I took a chance that I would get to see him, but I wanted the visit to be a surprise. I didn't want him to have time to prepare for our meeting, and that worked out to our advantage. My unannounced visit caught him off guard, and he had to come up with some answers and pretty quick. He didn't have time to think up a good story and cover his butt. The element of surprise in an investigation works pretty well, I've always found."

"You were lucky it worked out that way and were able to see him on short notice. You took a chance about that, but I'm glad it paid off. So you think you got the truth out of him without having to spend time asking a lot of questions?"

"Sure, it worked out just fine. All I had to do was show his secretary my badge. They're at the end of the semester with graduation approaching just like at Merryvale. I thought he might be busy, but was pretty sure he would be there. Of course, I thought I might have to wait around a while before I could see him; but he saw me right away. He wasn't exactly happy to see me—probably shocked that I'd actually made the trip up there. More than likely it finally dawned on him that he needed to cooperate with our investigation. I'll bet his conscience was probably bothering him too, and the old guy may have wanted to go ahead and get it off his chest, Jess. But whatever his thoughts were, here's his story. He claims he was unaware of anything irregular in Dr. Bowen's background. He had transcripts from Oxford, a list of academic publications, an entire background on the man. Absolutely no reason to question his identity. They thought they'd hired the real thing, an Oxford man. To say that he was shocked is to put it mildly. I thought the old guy was going to faint."

"So you believe him?"

"Yeah, I do for some reason. His response when I told him about our communication with Oxford and that the real Basil Bowen was dead seemed genuine. Of course, you could ask why he didn't check out the records with Oxford himself before the man was hired, but I didn't want to go there. He said they had the official transcripts from Oxford and that was all that was necessary along with his academic publications and letters of recommendation. You know, I don't think Merryvale checked that closely either, to tell the truth. But more than being concerned about the false identity,

I think the dean was terrified about writing a letter that made Dr. Bowen appear to be such an outstanding man. I believe he took the falsification of the truth in that letter very seriously and knew what kind of position that put him in. I'll explain what I mean about that later, Jess"

"In other words, Merryvale College took the dean's letter of recommendation and assumed that everything was in order. The documents were real, actually from Oxford, but unfortunately the man was not. This really complicates the case, Kevin. This guy could have been anybody with no telling how many people out to get him." Jess was trying to take it all in, wondering how they would ever be able to get to the bottom of this case. "What about his wife? Do you think she was in on it too?"

"First, I'm certain without a shadow of doubt that Merryvale College thought he was Dr. Basil Bowen, a graduate of Oxford University in England. They would have no reason to doubt it. But you're right. The murderer could be someone from his past that we know nothing about, someone from England or anywhere, for that matter. As for the wife, I'm not sure if she was in on the deception or not. But I have a gut feeling about all this. I'd be very surprised if the killer isn't right here on the campus."

"Identity theft, impersonation of a dead person! It's unbelievable that something like this could happen at Merryvale, Kevin."

"No, it isn't, Jess. It happens all the time. I admit we've been pretty lucky so far here in our little backwater, but there're numerous cases under investigation across the country right now. Someone assumes the identity of a person who has died, uses his Social Security number, and draws his pension. I'm not telling you anything new. I know you're aware that it's a serious problem. But what I'm wondering, and I'm sure the administration at Oxford is wondering, is how someone got the academic records, the official transcripts. It had to be an inside job. Well, that's their problem. They'll have to get to the bottom of it over there in England. Hopefully, Scotland Yard will be able to tie up the loose ends. I'm sure they take the security of their records pretty seriously, and they have offered their assistance if we need it. Our concern here is finding the murderer, and I think that will be a strictly local issue."

"I hate to tell you this, but I'm no closer than I was before you left, Kevin."

"I know, neither am I, but that's not the whole story. Let me explain what I meant about the dean being so nervous about that letter of recommendation. I picked up on that when I spoke to him on the phone. The reason they wanted to see the backside of Dr. Bowen is crucial to our case, and I think it narrows down our suspects. It seems our Dr. Bowen has a pretty strong sex drive. The professor likes to go both ways. He was carrying on with one of his students, a young man, and it became common knowledge on campus. The affair ended, but the tragic part is the boy committed suicide, and Dr. Bowen was encouraged to move on. Sound familiar?"

"Unfortunately, it does. But if you're thinking that Jud Sharp may have been in a similar position, I think you need to wait until you hear his story before you draw any conclusions. Tomorrow when you begin your interviews I think he will fill you in on the details and what led up to his breakdown."

Kevin looked at Jess. "You haven't been holding back information have you?"

"You know better than that, Kevin! How was I to know what you were going to find out in Virginia? Dr. Emily and I discussed this, and we decided we wanted to give Jud the opportunity to tell you face to face, in his own words, what Dr. Bowen's role was in this. If anything, what you discovered about Bowen's sexual preferences and his involvement with a student casts more suspicion on the wife, don't you think? Infidelity, jealousy, no matter how you look at it, it's a pretty powerful motive."

"Maybe, but now that you've brought up Elise Bowen again it will come as no surprise that she was not very popular up there either. It might be interesting to look into her background as well. I'm asking myself the same questions you are, and I can't help but wonder if she knew about him not being a graduate of Oxford University. Maybe she's not who she says she is either. Have you thought about that? But right now, all I want is a good night's sleep before we start the interviews tomorrow."

"Did Dean Watson tell you anything about the student that killed himself, Kevin? I imagine he didn't want to get into that, but I wonder if they still have his computer files. I assume he was an English major, but of course he could have been majoring in just about any subject."

"No, I didn't learn too much about him. Apparently they tried to conduct an investigation in a discreet manner. The boy left a handwritten suicide note. They checked his computer to see if they could get any more information about what was going on, but all the files had been erased. Why do you ask?"

"It was just a thought, curiosity, I guess. Trying to make a connection." Jess wanted Jud to be the one to explain to Kevin about Dr. Bowen's theft of intellectual property. He was almost certain the student in Virginia had been used in the same way. An expert might be able to retrieve those lost computer files. I'm getting ahead of myself, Jess thought, as he drove toward Merryvale. First things first.

As the car sped along the interstate, the traffic thinned out and the darkness had a soothing effect on Kevin. He leaned his head back on the passenger seat. Before long, he was sound asleep.

Jess wondered what Dr. Emily would make of this new information about Dr. Bowen's escapades in Virginia and the tragic result of his affair with a student. From Jess's point of view it validated Jud Sharp's claim about Dr. Bowen's abuse of power with him, and he couldn't get those missing computer files out of his mind.

It would be interesting to find out whether the young man who had committed suicide in Virginia had experienced the same problem with the professor taking his work and publishing it as his own. It would certainly make sense. If Dr. Bowen was pretending to be someone else and was in a position where academic publication was expected and part of the job description, then the pressure on him must have been tremendous. With an unlimited source of research information on the internet, it might not be too difficult to put together a decent lecture if you were not qualified, but to write an academic paper was another matter. This made Jess even more suspicious about the blank computer files in Virginia. No wonder Dr. Bowen had always impressed Jess as not being comfortable in his own skin.

After dropping Kevin off at his house, Jess was tempted to stop by Dr. Emily's, but as he drove by her home he saw that the lights were off. It was late; he would try to get some sleep himself and talk to her in the morning. Since regular classes weren't held during exam week, she would be in her office during the day unless she was giving a final. Not much could be done tonight, anyway. It would keep. He would drop by Tutwiler and fill her in with the information Kevin had gotten in Virginia first thing in the morning.

Kevin would be conducting the interviews in the conference room on the first floor of Tutwiler Hall, directly below Dr. Emily's office. It was a convenient location. Jess would be able to keep track of any new information in the case as the interviews were conducted, as well as keeping an eye on the English Department. But it was not going to be convenient for most people on campus, and it was going to be a difficult week for final exams. Students trying to concentrate on the end of the semester would be distracted and upset. He could sense the tension on campus. For everyone's sake, they needed to find the murderer.

He cruised around campus one last time before calling it a day. After he exited the main gate he drove slowly by Glenda's house. The lights were still on, and he was tempted to stop by for a visit and a glass of wine in the garden. He needed the comfort of a woman's arms around him and at least a kiss or two. He wouldn't spend the night, he thought; but, being realistic, he knew if he let himself ring the doorbell the evening would end that way. Better not, he muttered to himself. He would do the right thing and stick to his earlier resolve. That meant not socializing with anyone in the English Department until everyone had been questioned and the case was solved. It might take a while, but he had no doubt that there would be a break before long. At last, the facts were rapidly beginning to catch up with the man who had done so much damage to the college and the lives of two young men.

Finally at home, he stripped off his clothes, took a hot shower, and fell into bed. Sleep was not to come, however. He supposed the thought of Glenda had aroused his desire, and his sexual frustration was making it impossible to relax. As was his habit, he distracted himself by thinking about the case, by going back over again the sequence of events on the day of the Canterbury Faire. What had he seen that had been in any way out of the ordinary? He remembered Dr. Bowen had arrived late and was looking very ill at that early hour of the morning. Then he seemed to recollect that someone had said he had been sick most of the week. He would have to make inquiries about that. Maybe Dr. Emily had mentioned it, or Glenda.

The thought of Glenda brought back something else he had forgotten. Before Dr. Bowen had mounted up for the pilgrimage, he vaguely remembered that he seemed so unsteady on his feet that Glenda held him by the arm to give him some support. Elise had just created that awful scene saying she hated him. He must have been seriously ill even then. But there was something else that he couldn't remember. What was it? Finally, he drifted off into a restless sleep.

Across town, Kevin Mitchell was having difficulty sleeping as well. The short nap he'd taken in the car on the way home had taken the edge off his exhaustion and had given him a second wind. He tossed and turned going over in his mind the questions he would ask and what his approach would be when he started the interviews the next morning. His initial purpose was to get basic information: Where were you? What did you observe? Do you know anyone who had a grudge against Dr. Bowen?

Slowly his body began to relax and his eyelids began to droop. He would ask those questions tomorrow. He would put everyone at ease. That was his basic strategy. Put them at ease and they would begin to feel comfortable with him, more relaxed; and they would begin to give up more information, be more willing to talk. At least that was what he had always found during round one of the questioning of both witnesses and suspects. Somewhere in all that exhausting process he hoped he would learn something new. That's what he needed, more facts, so the pieces would begin to fall into place. Some law enforcement officers tried to intimidate witnesses. But making people nervous and uncomfortable was not his style. Giving his pillow a couple of jabs with his fist, he turned on his side and, with a sigh, Sheriff Kevin Mitchell finally slept.

Often he sat as justice in assize,
By patent or commission from the crown...
****

THE LAWYER
THE PROLOGUE OF THE CANTERBURY TALES
BY
GEOFFREY CHAUCER

Chapter 22

Dr. Emily Goldman loved her office in Julia Tutwiler Hall. It had become just as much her sanctuary over the years as the little Victorian house that she had purchased when she first started teaching at Merryvale College. Now those old houses surrounding the campus were selling for a premium; but, of course, she would never consider selling her beloved home, no matter how much she was offered.

Over the years she had traveled extensively, but had always returned to Merryvale College with a sense of homecoming. Twice while on sabbatical leave, she had spent several glorious months in the British Isles doing research; but as much as she had savored those trips, she was always ready to be back at home. She was more comfortable in her little house with the gingerbread trim than anywhere she could think of; and second to the comfort of her home, was the pleasure of working here in her office surrounded by the precious things that reminded her of the past. Today, however, she was restless and ill at ease.

Her conversation with Jess about her father's interest in botany had brought back so many memories of her youth in Chicago: the strict observance of Jewish tradition that was always maintained in her parents' house, her father's pride in her academic success at the University of Chicago, the love that she always felt from both of her parents, now long deceased, but living forever through her and her profession. Although she was not religious in a conventional sense, she still felt the value of observing the old traditions and their connection to her heritage.

Reflecting on the past was always a comfort for her; but today, the people she worked and socialized with were being questioned in the conference room directly below her; and this made her long for the peace of a deep religious faith. She raised her eyes and looked out across her beloved campus from the beautiful Palladian window that dominated the room. Silently, she prayed for justice and wisdom, and then her eyes came to rest on the menorah that had belonged to her grandparents.

As she studied its graceful shape and reflected on the tradition of the lighting of the candles, Dr. Emily felt a release of the tension that had enveloped her since early morning. Troubles were everywhere in this world, and her people had certainly had their share, she reflected. She reminded herself that it was essential that she remain calm and brave no matter what discoveries lay ahead in the investigation. The way of the world could not be overcome, and the evil that was always present had to be faced with strength of character.

In the room below Dr. Goldman, Sheriff Kevin Mitchell was feeling anything but calm as he looked across the conference table at Elise Bowen. She was elegantly dressed in a simple black dress set off with an opera length, single strand of pearls. Proper attire for a widow in mourning, he supposed; but for a woman who had recently lost her husband, she seemed not in the least touched by sadness. Instead her haughty manner and nasty attitude seemed to have increased since the last time Kevin had a conversation with her. It took a supreme effort on his part to be civil.

"Mrs. Bowen, let me again say that all of us extend our deepest sympathy to you and your family, but there are some questions that simply have to be cleared up before I can allow you to leave and return to Virginia."

Elise's eyes roamed around the room, looking everywhere except directly at Kevin. "Well, at least I've been given permission to claim my husband's remains and make arrangements for his interment. What other questions could you possibly have, Sheriff Mitchell? I've already told you that I had nothing to do with Basil's death. We've been over this until I feel quite ill!"

"I'm sorry to have to continue to ask these questions, Mrs. Bowen, but I believe you said Dr. Bowen had not been feeling well for most of the week leading up to the Faire? Do you have any idea what the problem was?"

"Of course I do. I'm not going to cover up for him now that he's dead. Part of Basil's problem was that he was drinking heavily. Every night since that wretched student of his attempted suicide, he had been drinking like a fish. He'd been able to hide his drinking since we arrived in Merryvale, but after that boy . . ." Elise thought perhaps she had said too much and she caught herself before she said more.

Kevin found he was getting nowhere with his kind, gentle approach. The woman's arrogance was getting under his skin. He changed tactics and with an abrupt voice asked, "Did you know your husband was a fraud, Mrs. Bowen? That he was not a graduate of Oxford University, or at least we don't believe he was, and that his name wasn't Basil Bowen? In fact, we've yet to discover his true identity. Who was he really? What was his real name?"

Elise looked blankly at Kevin Mitchell. "What are you talking about? What are you saying? You must be out of your mind!"

"I've been in touch with officials at Oxford University in England and have discovered some rather shocking news. Your husband probably never even attended Oxford. It seems the real Basil Bowen died three years ago. Were you aware of your husband's true identity and the fraud he was committing, not just at Merryvale College, but in Virginia as well? Have you been helping him play out this charade, Mrs. Bowen?"

Elise continued to stare blankly at Kevin Mitchell remaining perfectly still. Kevin expected her to make some sort of reply, but she didn't say a word. Most of the color drained from her face, leaving her carefully applied makeup looking like the paint on the face of a china doll. Her eyes blinked slowly several times before they closed completely and she slumped sideways in her chair.

Thinking fast, Kevin jumped to his feet and managed to grab her before she toppled over. Holding Elise Bowen awkwardly in his arms, Kevin cursed. "Holy shit!" He shouted for Jess Thornton who was stationed outside the door of the conference room.

"Jess, call an ambulance!" Jess was already dialing 911 on his cell phone as he burst into the room and rushed toward them.

"What happened, Kevin? She looks pale as a ghost.

Kevin lowered Elise gently to the floor and checked her pulse. "I didn't handle that very well, Jess. Shock, I guess. I told her Basil was a fake and that he'd probably never attended Oxford, at least I suppose he hadn't—that the real Basil died three years ago. I guess it was kind of brutal of me; but, damn it, she just rubs me the wrong way!" Belatedly, Kevin tried to look contrite.

Jess quickly took in the situation and attempted to reassure his friend. "Don't worry about it, Kevin. We're only human and that woman . . ." His voice trailed off as he thought better of what he was going to say.

Elise seemed to be coming around by the time the ambulance arrived to take her to the hospital. Her eyelids flickered, and she looked at Jess and Kevin with an uncomprehending stare. The paramedics placed her on a gurney and wheeled her quickly out of the room. Jess followed them to the ambulance and after watching it drive away, returned to Kevin, who was still looking a bit guilty. It was obvious he still felt he had been a little too rough on her. Usually the epitome of professionalism, the strain was beginning to take its toll, even on Sheriff Kevin Mitchell.

"Just a precautionary measure, I would imagine. The paramedics seem to think she simply fainted. They said her vital signs seem to be okay. To be fair, she's been under considerable strain, probably not eating properly. Don't feel guilty about it, Kevin. You were just doing your job. Besides, she strikes me as the kind of woman who's a lot tougher than she looks," Jess remarked.

Kevin paced around the conference room table. "Either she had no idea that her husband was a fake, or she's one of the best actresses I've seen in a long time. Who's next on the list? You might as well send them in." Kevin flipped through his notebook until he came to a clean page.

"Jud Sharp is waiting just outside, I'll bring him in. I'm sure this little drama hasn't helped his nerves any. Just listen to his story, Kevin. Dr. Goldman and I think this will shed a lot of light on what might have led to Dr. Bowen's murder, especially since we know about the suicide in Virginia."

"Don't worry, Jess. I'll treat him with kid gloves. I promise I won't make him faint."

Jess smiled weakly. "I know you will, Kevin."

"Sorry about that. There's not really anything to joke about. I just want to get to the bottom of this case, damn it; and there're too many angles!"

"Take it easy, Kevin. I feel the same way. I'll leave you to it, but I think I'll hang around outside for a while longer if that's okay with you. Dr. Goldman, bless her heart, wanted me to bring Jud up to her office after he talked to you."

Kevin walked to the conference room door. "Tell Jud to come on in."

Jess stepped back into the hall. "Sure. See you later."

Once Jud was settled in a chair and the door was shut softly by Jess Thornton, Kevin did as he promised and very gently began to ask a few questions about Jud's studies. Jud seemed to relax; and, gradually, with Kevin listening intently and taking notes, Jud told him exactly what he had told Dr. Emily. He explained about Dr. Bowen's sexual advances, the theft of his academic work and its subsequent publication, and finally the threatened blackmail to keep him out of graduate school.

As the story unfolded, Kevin grew angrier by the minute, and he struggled to maintain his professional demeanor. It made his blood boil to hear how this young college student had been abused. As he studied Jud's face, he knew in his gut that he could not possibly be the killer. Jud may have been disillusioned and depressed about what must have been the worst betrayal a young person could imagine, so much so that he attempted to take his own life, but he was not the sort to harm another person. Sheriff Kevin Mitchell was a pretty good judge of character, and he was sure that the young man sitting across from him was telling the truth. Unfortunately, the district attorney thought he was a prime suspect even though the evidence was circumstantial. Kevin felt sick at heart. He was afraid if the district attorney had his way; Jud Sharp was very much in danger of being charged with the murder of Dr. Basil Bowen.

Lo now, the oak that has long nourishing
Even from the time that it begins to spring,
And has so long a life, as we may see,
Yet at the last all wasted is the tree.
****

THE KNIGHT'S TALE
THE CANTERBURY TALES
BY
GEOFFREY CHAUCER

Chapter 23

The interviews continued for the rest of the morning and into the late afternoon. Sheriff Mitchell had taken meticulous notes and recorded critical portions of the interviews. All had gone as he expected. No one knew anything about what happened; no one could imagine why anyone would want to harm Dr. Bowen; no one saw anything suspicious. They all expressed shock and revulsion at the murder.

The afternoon passed slowly; it was almost dark before Kevin was satisfied that he had asked every pertinent question he could think of. He had interviewed and carefully questioned every faculty member in the English Department, the administrative staff, and all of the student assistants. The only thing he had established was that Dr. Bowen had been unpopular with most of the students and was avoided if at all possible; most of the young people admitted this reluctantly. They simply didn't like the man. They found him hard to approach about academic matters, and his arrogance had made them feel uncomfortable when they were around him. Not surprisingly, they spent as little time as possible in his company.

After interviewing the student assistants, Kevin moved on to the faculty and staff. He chose his questions carefully hoping to catch someone in an inconsistency in their answers, but straightforward answers were given about Dr. Bowen. No one seemed to like the man; he was difficult and arrogant, but no one on the faculty seemed to have a motive for murder, with the possible exception of the two professors Dr. Bowen had treated so badly.

Dr. Greer and Dr. Adams were both obviously nervous during their interviews, but they were both so mild mannered it seemed ludicrous to even consider the possibility that either one would be capable of murder. On the morning of the Faire, both of them said they had stayed well away from Dr. Bowen as he and Elise argued; and none of the other witnesses could place either one of them anywhere near him. Kevin couldn't see how either one of them could have given him the poison. Besides, without any physical evidence there were just so many questions that could be asked, and this was seriously hampering the case.

Simply too much time had passed between the Faire and the completion of the coroner's report of poisoning by hemlock for any forensic evidence to be gathered from the scene, Kevin realized. Students had walked back and forth to class over the pilgrimage route. Several heavy spring rains had washed clean the ground around the stable, and the horses themselves had trampled all over the area. The forensic team had gone over the route with a fine-toothed comb, but had come up empty handed.

To make matters worse, they had found no trace of the flask Dr. Bowen was seen drinking from that morning. At least the flask would have provided the police with something to go on, especially if it contained residue of the hemlock. Several of the witnesses remembered seeing Dr. Bowen drinking from it while he was on horseback and naturally assumed it belonged to him.

If Elsie's statement about his drinking habits was true, it probably was his; but it was also possible someone had given it to him. Unfortunately, the flask was lost somehow during the confusion created by Dr. Bowen's fall from his horse and the subsequent hours of revelry taking place at the Faire. They needed to recover that flask.

Kevin doubted that it would ever be found. Nothing was certain in this case, he thought. He was scheduled to meet with the district attorney on the following morning to give a report of his findings, and he basically had nothing new to tell him, no hard evidence. Murder by person or persons unknown was not going to sit very well with the DA.

In the meantime, he hoped Jess Thornton and Dr. Goldman would miraculously come up with something that would help them move forward. Without additional evidence, he was afraid the DA would still be focused on Jud Sharp as the most likely suspect, the one with the strongest motive. He had to admit that the motive was clearly there, but without any evidence he didn't see how they could arrest him. If he was arrested, the Grand Jury could possibly bring in an indictment, although that seemed doubtful; but it could happen.

It was hard to predict what a jury would do if the case went to trial. Kevin thought it would be difficult to get a conviction based on nothing but circumstantial evidence, but once proceedings began anything could happen. Juries could be unpredictable. Although he was positive Jud Sharp was not the murderer, he believed that an arrest and the ordeal of standing trial would destroy the boy emotionally after all he had been through. Kevin didn't want to see that happen.

He had to present the case to the district attorney in a way that would take some of the focus off of Jud Sharp. That would be his strategy, and he hoped the DA could be convinced that Jud was an unlikely suspect. It might appear that he had the strongest motive for murdering Dr. Bowen; but there were still a number of people who would not grieve for him, who would certainly not be sorry to see him dead, and could not be ruled out as suspects. This was the only thing he could think of at the moment.

If he had been a betting man, Kevin would have put all of his chips on Elise Bowen. She certainly had the opportunity, and their unhappy marriage seemed as good a motive as any, but he still had questions about the type of poison used. If Elise had decided to get rid of her husband, why would she pick hemlock? Arsenic, good old rat poison, would have worked just as well. Of course it would have taken longer; but it would have done the job.

Dr. Emily had spent most of the day in her office asking herself the same questions. She was grading final exams without making a great deal of progress; her mind continued to go back to Dr. Bowen and the poison used to kill him. She had talked to Jud briefly after he had finished answering Kevin Mitchell's questions and had reassured him that all would be well. He seemed confident that he had answered the questions to Kevin's satisfaction, and had told the Sheriff the whole story, not holding anything back. He said he felt a great sense of relief at finally telling his story to the police.

After Jud left her office, she tried to clear her mind and continue to grade the student papers. It was slow-going. She couldn't forget that the questioning of her colleagues and friends was taking place on the floor below, and she found it very difficult to concentrate. It must be a very unsettling feeling for them, she thought. No doubt none of them would have ever imagined having to answer questions about a murder, especially the murder of the head of the English Department.

Merryvale College was not used to such drama; and, of course, the press was very much in evidence outside the building, waiting for what little information they could get as witnesses emerged. From time to time she paused as she read one student essay after another. She finally gave up and allowed her mind to wander as she once again tried to think back about the day of the Faire. Had there been anything that she had seen or heard that didn't ring true or that seemed out of place?

There was still something in the back of her mind that continued to nag away at her, but she couldn't put her finger on it. What was it, she thought? It could possibly be something of great importance, but then again she wondered if her imagination was running away with her. It had all started with that dream. She closed her eyes and tried to remember the details of the terrifying nightmare she had a few weeks before the Faire. She could see the face of the man as he fell from his horse; the image of his open eyes staring at the heavens as he lay on the ground was vivid.

She was certain the face had been that of Dr. Bowen dressed in a medieval costume as he played the part of the host. The nightmare still haunted her, but revealed nothing about the very real death of her department head. Besides, it was simply a dream, wasn't it? A sense of unease invaded her usually orderly mind. She was not a superstitious woman, but it was unsettling to think that the dream had been some kind of premonition. It was too real, too much like reality. She hoped she was wrong, but she felt a chill and sensed there would be more violence on her beloved campus before this whole business was over.

She picked up another exam to grade and read over the first few paragraphs, knowing she was not giving it her full attention. Her students were getting off easy this semester, she reflected. Her mind drifted back to the conference room on the floor below. She needed to meet with Jess Thornton and Kevin Mitchell as soon as possible. She wanted to know how the questioning had gone. In talking over the case with them, it was possible that something would be mentioned that would jog her memory; and she would be able to remember what was troubling her and whom it concerned.

After her last paper was graded, she sat at her desk and once again started to make a list of the people she thought could have possibly wanted Basil Bowen dead. Elise Bowen was at the top, but in order to be fair, she found herself putting Jud's name down next, if only because he had an extremely strong motive. Then she felt guilty since she was certain Jud had nothing to do with the murder, scratched out his name, and threw the paper in the wastebasket by her desk. She must have made a dozen lists by now, and none of them had led anywhere.

As she packed her briefcase for the walk home, she hoped she would run into Jess and Kevin on her way out. It must appear to be a casual encounter, and then she could somehow get them both to her house to talk things over. It seemed absurd to her that she had to think like this, but both men were right in continually reminding her that there was still a murderer among them. As luck would have it, both men were preparing to leave as she walked down the stairs to the first floor.

"Dr. Emily!" Jess raised his hand in salute as she descended the stairs. "Let me give you a lift home. You're working late tonight."

"Thank you, Jess. It's all those final exams. I would be grateful for a ride home."

As Jess opened the car door he whispered in her ear. "Kevin is going to park his car on a side street and come in through your back garden. We need to talk over everything we know right away, and put our heads together. But we still need to be careful."

"That's what I was hoping we could do, Jess. And don't worry, I'm taking every precaution. I'm being very careful and locking my doors at night." After negotiating their way around the press still hanging around Tutwiler Hall and ignoring their questions, Dr. Emily put her briefcase on the floor of the police car and slid in as Jess carefully closed the door behind her.

"You better check your windows too and don't forget your seatbelt," he grinned.

"Don't tell me you would give me a ticket for a seatbelt violation!" she laughed.

Later, after Kevin arrived, they settled into Dr. Emily's living room with all the shades down and the curtains drawn, took out their notes, and began to go over what they knew for certain. Unfortunately, it wasn't much. All three agreed that of the possible suspects, Jud Sharp had a strong motive, but they also thought that Elise Bowen was also at the top of the list. They had no idea what the DA might be thinking and felt the urgency of coming up with evidence that would point to another suspect, or at least find some way to clear Jud's name.

Jess thought that they had been too quick in ruling out Dr. Greer and Adams as serious suspects. Both professors had been deeply hurt and belittled by Dr. Bowen. It might just be possible that one of them had the opportunity to give him the poison without being seen, maybe prior to his arrival at the Faire.

Then the question was raised about the location of the flask. Was the flask attached to the saddle of Dr. Bowen's mount perhaps? Some flasks had a wrist strap that could have been hooked over the horn of a saddle. It would've only taken a moment to switch the flask on the saddle during the time he was arguing with Elise. The possibilities were endless, but no one had seen either Dr. Greer or Dr. Adams anywhere near Dr. Bowen on the morning of the Faire. At least it had not been mentioned so far.

It was painful for Dr. Emily to even consider these two highly regarded professors as murder suspects; but when a person's whole life was dedicated to a particular academic profession, emotions could run high. To question or ridicule a life's work would be considered an unforgivable insult.

"I'm beginning to think we need to call Dr. Adams and Dr. Greer back in for a few more questions," Kevin said. "We only have their word that they were nowhere near Dr. Bowen as they were all getting ready to start the procession. If I remember correctly, they said they both wanted to stay as far away from the Bowen's argument as possible; but they could have been wandering around for a good while without attracting any attention. I believe they were together most of the time. Maybe someone saw something unusual. I'll check that out."

"Yes, I imagine they have been brought together by their conflict with Dr. Bowen, and that might lead somewhere, but I can't believe that either of them would plan to murder him." Dr. Emily shook her head in disbelief.

"What if they were afraid of losing their teaching positions here at the college?" Jess injected.

"Impossible." Dr. Emily replied. "Dr. Adams and Dr. Greer are both tenured professors. Now they may have been afraid of being discredited in some way. It's hard to know what Dr. Bowen may have said to them in private. After all, he convinced Jud he could ruin his academic career."

Sheriff Mitchell's cell phone rang; he stepped into the kitchen to take the call. Dr. Emily and Jess sat fidgeting until he returned, unwilling to continue the discussion until he was back in the room and hoping that the call was something new about the case. Kevin's displeasure was written all over his face as he rejoined them. His face was slightly flushed and his struggle to control his frustration was evident.

"Elise Bowen has been released from the hospital, and her attorney has demanded that she be allowed to return to Virginia. She will keep us notified of her whereabouts and will return for further questioning if it's considered necessary."

"Well, there goes my prime suspect," Jess frowned. "The public argument they had at the Faire and her saying that she hated him in front of all those people put her at the top of my list."

"Don't worry, Jess. She'll be subpoenaed to appear and answer more questions under oath if we ever go to trial with this. She's been instructed to keep in touch with law enforcement here and not to leave the country under any circumstances. The DA couldn't continue to keep her in Alabama without some evidence that she either committed the murder or was an accessory to her husband's death. But don't get me wrong. I don't have any sympathy for the woman either."

Kevin reached for the pack of cigarettes in his pocket and then thought better of it. "The more I think about it, the more I think that was one big act this afternoon. I don't believe that little lady fainted at all. It was a trick. I've seen kids do it when they don't get their way. She simply held her breath until she passed out. I'll admit I was pretty abrupt with my questioning. When I told her Basil was a fraud, she just sat there looking at me and didn't say a word. I believe she faked the whole thing. I'm sure she regained consciousness well before the paramedics arrived, but she pretended to still be out of it. The hospital found nothing wrong with her once they got her there and checked her over. I'll bet you anything she knew all along that old Basil was a fraud. That's how she got away with treating him the way she did. He knew she had a powerful weapon to hold over him, metaphorically, that is."

"It would be interesting to know if she knew about his fake identity before she married him or found out about it afterwards," Dr. Emily mused. "Can you imagine, thinking you've married an Oxford man and then finding out it was a lie, that he was someone else. It must have been a terrible strain on both of them and on their marriage. And then, of course, there was his bisexuality. Another blow to her self-esteem, I would think."

"That would put a strain on any marriage," Kevin said.

"Wait a moment. It's coming back to me now—what I've been trying to remember." Dr. Emily began to twist a ring on the finger of her left hand. "We heard about the suicide of the young man in Virginia after your trip up there, didn't we Kevin?"

"Yes, Dr. Emily, according to the dean, that's why Dr. Bowen was asked to leave, but they agreed to give him a letter of recommendation to another institution. That way there would be no scandal, and they were covering their backsides. Bad luck for us."

"But although the relationship with the young man was out in the open in Virginia, no one here knew about it until the dean in Virginia told you, correct? Dr. Emily gripped the arms of her chair and looked from one man to another. "And neither of you shared that information with anyone except me."

Both men nodded their heads, not sure where this was going, but certain that Dr. Emily was on the track of some important bit of evidence.

"Since the time frame has been established I want to relate a conversation I had with an employee of our college, an employee of the English Department to be exact. After Jud Sharp's suicide attempt, which mercifully was not successful, I thought it was very strange that he had signed up for a part in the Faire. Be patient with me. I know we've talked about this before. An employee of the college confirmed that Jud had indeed signed up for the part that very morning. It didn't make sense to me at the time, and I couldn't figure it out. I've never forgotten it." Dr. Emily had a puzzled look on her face. "I asked myself, why would a young man sign up for a part, a role he had looked forward to playing, and then attempt to take his own life that very afternoon?"

"Yes, I remember discussing this with you Dr. Emily. It troubled you until you heard the full story from Jud and learned about the threat Dr. Bowen had made about keeping him out of graduate school." Jess nodded.

"That's what I have been trying to remember. Someone else on this campus knew about the suicide in Virginia before you found out anything about it, Kevin!"

Kevin was on his feet, pacing from one side of the room to the other. "As far as I know, no one on this campus knew about the other suicide; and even if he had, without knowing that Dr. Bowen was stealing student work, impersonating someone else, and all the other tricks he was up to, it wouldn't have meant anything to anyone here at Merryvale anyway. Let's face it. Students do try to kill themselves for a number of reasons. It happens on just about every campus from time to time. The difference in this case is that there was enough of a connection between the poor kid in Virginia and Dr. Bowen that the dean was anxious to get rid of his Oxford Don. In other words, he smelled a rat!"

Dr. Emily nodded in agreement. "But let's go back and think very carefully about what this means. The morning following Jud's suicide attempt, one of our employees made a remark to me, but I really didn't pay too much attention. It didn't register at the time. But I haven't forgotten it, and now I wonder about its significance." Max was sitting at her feet studying her face. He gave a sharp little yip of frustration.

"For goodness sake, Dr. Emily! Tell us what it was and who said it!" Kevin was about to lose what little patience he had left. "Look at Max. I think he knows exactly what we're talking about!"

Dr. Emily had a stricken look on her face. "Glenda. It was Glenda," Dr. Emily said in a rather plaintive voice. "She seemed so upset that morning when I came into the office. She was upset about Jud and had been crying a little, I think. We talked about what happened, and then she said, 'Just like the other one—or that other boy.' I can't remember her exact words." I said, 'What did you say? Not sure I had heard her correctly."

"What was her response?" Kevin asked.

"She was speaking rather softly as if to herself. She said, 'Oh, never mind' or something of that nature. She didn't elaborate. I assumed it had made her think about someone else, some other tragedy. Anyway, she became a little more emotional and excused herself to go into the ladies' room to repair her makeup."

"Where is Glenda from?" Kevin asked. "I know she started working at the college about the same time Dr. Bowen came—the beginning of the fall semester, wasn't it?"

Not a word was said for a few moments. They were each lost deep in thought. Max looked from one face to another cocking his head to one side.

Jess Thornton looked dazed. "Virginia. She told me she was from Virginia."

"Yes, I was afraid of that." Dr. Emily's eyes were moist with tears. "That was what I'd been trying to remember. When I learned of the suicide of the boy involved with Dr. Bowen, it finally brought Glenda's remark back to mind. At the time I simply thought that she was talking about some poor boy from long ago, perhaps something she had read about in the paper.

Now I wonder if she'd been reminded of him after Jud tried to kill himself. Kevin, I'm afraid you're going to have to find out how Glenda and that unfortunate young man were connected."

"I'll start making inquiries first thing in the morning," Kevin sighed. "God, I hate this!"

"It's been a long day," Jess said. "Let's all try to get some sleep. Whatever the connection might be, it can wait until tomorrow." His face was pale as he picked up his hat and walked with Kevin to the front door of the little Victorian house.

Three times she'd journeyed to Jerusalem;
And many a foreign stream she'd had to stem;
At Rome she'd been, and she'd been in Boulogne,
In Spain at Santiago, and at Cologne.
She could tell much of wandering by the way...

****

THE WIFE OF BATH
THE PROLOGUE OF THE CANTERBURY TALES
BY
GEOFFREY CHAUCER

Chapter 24

Glenda was in a wistful mood as she sat outside her little cottage watching the moon rise above her garden fence. She missed Jess Thornton more than she imagined she would, but she wasn't looking for a permanent relationship and realized early on that he wasn't either. That was fine with her. She understood that Jess couldn't afford to socialize with her during a murder investigation; however, she sensed it would be difficult to pick up where they had left off. The relationship, which had been strictly a physical one, was probably over; but she had enjoyed the warmth, the companionship, the sex, and having someone to feel close to. She wasn't feeling sorry for herself, exactly, since she had grown accustomed to being alone and most of the time preferred it that way. It was only when she allowed herself the luxury of becoming close to someone that she found it hard to go back to being single.

Tonight she felt calmer than she had in a long time. She had answered Sheriff Kevin Mitchell's questions that afternoon to his satisfaction, she supposed, revealing nothing. She told him she had no idea who could possibly want to harm Dr. Bowen and felt confident that he had believed her and that the interview was just the routine questioning of everyone in the department. Now that she had accomplished what she had set out to do, she was feeling let down, she had to admit to herself, and feeling a bit of regret. Regret for everything that was lost.

She had grown to love her little cottage and her job at Merryvale College and wished that things could have turned out differently. It was as if she had been possessed by someone she didn't know. If only she had been able to suppress that powerful emotion, revenge; but of course, it was too late to go back now. She had loved her nephew and was certain that one day he would have been a teacher, perhaps even a professor; but all of that had ended with his death.

He was the child of her sister, who had died young, the closest thing she would ever have to a child of her own. She had taken care of him after her sister's death and financed his college career, a career that had just begun, she thought. It had made no difference to her that he was gay. She'd loved him unconditionally. All the blame for his death, all of her rage and fury, was placed on the man she hated more than anyone else. Her nephew had told her about him; and she had asked the usual questions about a man she had never met, who had no idea she even existed. But she knew who he was and had held him accountable. He was the man who had damaged her nephew to such an extent that he must have felt he couldn't continue to live.

Glenda would see him rot in hell! What kind of monster would do that, she wondered; and wasn't it her right to make certain he never manipulated the mind of another young person? She knew she wouldn't have a hard time finding him, even though she had never seen the bastard. When she discovered he'd left Virginia, his reputation tarnished, after her nephew's suicide; she asked around campus and found out where he had gone. Campus gossip had made it easy for her to trace him to Alabama.

Without looking back and without a moment's hesitation, she had made plans and followed him to

Merryvale College, not really sure what her next step would be, but determined to get even. On her arrival, as luck would have it, she found there was an administrative vacancy in the English Department. She took it as a sign, applied for the job, and was hired. It wasn't a demanding job, and all that was required was that she bide her time until she could settle the score.

She had never expected to work so closely with him, and at first that had been difficult, but she had always been a good actress. She pretended to have escaped from the corporate grind in a big city, and began to play the role of administrative assistant. Things had just drifted along. She settled in and began to enjoy her new home and the college, but never stopped looking for an opportunity. Then Jud Sharp's attempt on his life had strengthened her resolve and made her realize the necessity of moving quickly before he did more harm or before she lost her nerve. The Faire had given her the perfect opportunity.

Sitting quietly in her garden, reflecting on all that had happened since her move to Merryvale, she heard the footsteps, the click of heels, even before the side gate to her garden opened, and knew instantly who it was and why she was there. Now she sat staring at the wife of the man who had caused her and so many others so much grief.

"You know why I'm here, don't you?" Elise said.

"Well, I have a pretty good idea. I imagine you have stopped by to bid me a fond farewell before you head back to Virginia. A pity you had to hang around here so long." The note of sarcasm in Glenda's voice went right over Elise's head.

"Don't be silly. You know very well why I came."

"Why don't you sit down for a few minutes? It's been a difficult day for all of us, and you must be feeling a little ragged around the edges after your trip to the hospital." Since they had never exchanged more than a few words, Glenda was puzzled why Elise had decided to pay her a visit at the end of such a stressful day. At first she thought Elise was in a rather hostile mood, but now she wasn't certain. Perhaps they'd given her medication at the hospital, and it had gone to her head.

Elise sank into one of the garden chairs across from Glenda. "Isn't it rather dark to be doing paperwork out here?"

Earlier in the evening, Glenda had balanced her checkbook and taken care of a few bills as she sat in the comfort of the garden. The paperwork was still spread out on the table before them. "I've been sitting here for a long time admiring the moon and thinking things over. There's only one thing I know for certain in this world," Glenda said. "Debts have to be paid."

"Well said." Elise smiled. "Don't you think it's about time you paid yours?" Elise's speech was slightly slurred.

Glenda wondered if she'd had a few drinks on top of whatever medication they had given her. "I'm not sure I know what you're talking about or why you're here; but as far as I'm concerned, I can call all of my accounts paid in full, Elise"

She wasn't really sure why she had made that remark. It was dropping a hint, an innuendo, and she regretted revealing even that much. She began to wonder if Elise hated Basil as much as she did. Judging from her behavior on the day of the fair, it seemed highly likely.

"I know exactly what you mean, Glenda. No need to continue to play the part. I've known who you are for a long time. You must have forgotten that I know people in Virginia, and I asked around. It took a while, of course, but I found out not too long before the Faire that you're the aunt of that boy who killed himself. I'm sorry about that. Sorry for your loss."

"I refuse to discuss my nephew with you. What do you want Elise?"

"I think you know what I want, Glenda. You see, I was standing very close to both of you on the day of the Faire, and I saw what you did. I saw you give Basil a drink out of your flask. He drank it right down. He'd drink anything with alcohol. That was what was wrong with him that morning. He wasn't sick with a virus like he'd told everyone that week, just terribly hung over. He had his own flask with him, you know. When he fell off his horse I just thought he was drunk. But I know better than that."

"What does that prove, Elise? So you saw him drink out of my flask. Lots of people were carrying flasks that day."

"That's not the only thing that I know. It was very foolish of you, Glenda, to keep the hemlock here in your garden. Her gaze rested on the large vibrant plants with their tumbrils of white flowers growing close to Glenda's back garden wall. The moon was casting its light on the tiny blossoms, and they seemed to glow with a radiance that Glenda hadn't noticed before.

"I knew you gave it to him, even before I saw it here. It grows everywhere in the South—on the sides of the roads, in pastures—hell, you can even order the seeds on the internet. The seeds are the most poisonous. You should've just ordered those. Saved you the trouble of growing it yourself . . ." Her voice trailed off.

Glenda thought for a moment that Elise was going to pass out. She put her head down on the table as she continued to talk. "I understand that you did it for yourself, to get even with him; but I'm grateful to you. You did me a big favor, Glenda. You got rid of him for me. If you hadn't poisoned him, I would have eventually killed him myself."

She took a deep breath, raised her head off the table, and leaned back in her chair. She seemed to be breathing a little easier. "I've suffered from panic attacks all my life. It makes you feel like you're going to die. I know you don't care, but I'm not going to let this one stop me from telling you what you need to do now, Glenda. I imagine you already know. You know the cops will never be able to prove anything. They have no idea where the hemlock came from, much less who gave it to Basil. By the way, you should've already dug that stuff up and burned it. What were you thinking? Of course, now it's just our little secret."

"I'm going to ask you for the last time, Elise. What do you want? Money, I suppose."

"How'd you ever guess? Now you know your bills aren't paid in full after all." She looked at Glenda with a mercenary gleam in her eyes. "It's obvious you have money. A secretary working for a small school like this can't lease such a nice house and live the way you do. I was curious. I started asking around. I know something about the family you come from. People from Virginia know all about the old families." Elise seemed to sag in her chair, but her voice became shrill.

"That bastard Basil liked to take advantage of his students, especially the young men. But you know what's worse than that? He was poor! Said he was from an old family that went back to the Norman Conquest. What a joke! Just all part of the role he was trying to play, I guess, but it sure took me in. That's right. I believed his lies to begin with, but it didn't take me long to find out about him."

"So now you want money to keep quiet. Is that it?"

"Sure, why not? That way we both come out ahead. I can get out of this stinking place and get on with my life; and you can do whatever you want, just as long as you take care of your good friend, Elise."

"You have it all figured out don't you? You realize that the police won't believe you. You can't prove anything you've said to me tonight. You had just as much of a motive to kill Basil as I did. And then you were stupid enough to make a public display of yourself on the day of the Faire by telling the world how much you hated him. Why should they believe you?"

"I suppose you think I have too much pride to go to the police and tell them about Basil's affair with your nephew, Glenda. That wouldn't bother me at all after what he put me through. Oh, they know all about Dr.

Basil Bowen. Sheriff Mitchell told me this afternoon they found out that Basil had stolen the identity of a dead man from Oxford. The English authorities are checking in to that. In other words, he wasn't who he said he was, Glenda. He was a fraud; and he fooled me just as he fooled everyone else."

Glenda couldn't help but show her surprise at this bit of information. "You mean he was playing a part. Not a real professor from Oxford?"

"The bastard was a fake! Don't you see? I'll never be able to hold my head up again in Virginia. I can hear the whispers now. There goes Elise Bowen, the woman whose husband was murdered, who pretended to be from the British upper class!" Elise seemed to be about to lose her grip on her panic attack. She began to breathe rapidly, and Glenda thought she might hyperventilate.

She sat calmly and watched Elise as she struggled to gain control. The full moon lit the garden enough for her to clearly see the expression on Elise's face. She appeared helpless in the throes of the attack, her face deathly pale in the moonlight.

Glenda's paperwork, checkbook, and letter opener were lying there on the garden table. It would be so easy to kill her now, she thought. For one brief moment she looked at the letter opener. It wouldn't be hard to insert that sharp point into her neck. Then, what? Bury her in the garden and try to go on with her life at the college? No, of course not, she thought. It would never work. If the police knew about Basil Bowen being a fraud they would be conducting an investigation in Virginia and Oxford. They hadn't gotten very far in their investigation here, but they would in Virginia. They would eventually find out about the suicide of her nephew and make the connection.

Once that connection was made, they would be knocking at her door, asking more questions. It wouldn't be long before the whole ugly story came out, and they would arrest her for the murder. Elise Bowen's silence would be worthless. But for now, all she wanted was to get the woman out of her garden before she passed out.

"I left a sealed letter with my attorney. It's with my will and is to be opened only after I'm dead. It names you, Glenda, as the one who murdered Basil. It explains what I saw on the day of the Faire and that you grew the hemlock here in your garden to poison him. Unlike Basil, I won't be so easy to get rid of." Once again Elise seemed to be able to bring her breathing almost back to a normal level.

"I don't believe a word you're saying Elise. No self-respecting attorney would be a part of something like that. He could be disbarred for withholding that kind of information."

"Oh, he doesn't know what the letter says. I simply gave him instructions to place it with my will in my safety deposit box. He has power of attorney over my affairs. He's the only other person who has a key to the box. You see, I've thought of everything."

Glenda realized what she had long suspected, that Elise was totally amoral. She was willing to do anything, including blackmail, for her own personal gain. Once again, Glenda thought about killing her. To some extent, she blamed her for what had happened to her nephew, just because she was Basil Bowen's wife, she supposed. Surely, Elise knew what Basil was up to with his students, and she should share in the blame. Her precious nephew had killed himself because of that scum, and she was sure Bowen had driven him to it. She didn't know all of the details, but she knew enough to be sure. Elise was no better than he was, she thought. That was all she needed to know.

Now she hated Elise almost as much as she had Basil. Could this woman have prevented that tragedy by speaking out? Of course, there was no way of knowing for sure, so she held herself back. She couldn't inflict bodily harm on this creature, she thought. It had to stop somewhere. Her purpose had been accomplished.

The fraudulent Basil Bowen and his power to corrupt had been revealed, and she had taken him out of this world in a symbolic way that was fitting to his crime.

There was only one thing left that she couldn't control. She didn't want her choice of poison to be misunderstood. She hoped that when people discussed Basil Bowen's death he wouldn't be compared in any way to Socrates, that noble teacher who had gone to his death with dignity, condemned for corrupting the youth of Athens. She hoped Basil would be remembered for the exact crime of which Socrates was falsely accused; and to understand the method she used to kill him fit the crime so perfectly, a death sentence administered for the corruption of youth.

Once it became public knowledge about his false identity and his academic plagiarism, Glenda thought most educated people would draw a connection with her choice of poison and applaud her method of execution. They might even think that not only was it well thought out, but that justice had been served. Perhaps then her terrible deed would be understood.

No, she would not kill Elise, even though she could do it so easily. She would play along with the blackmail attempt. If nothing else, just to get the woman out of her life. "How much do you want," she asked? "I could write you a check. I don't keep a great deal of cash around the house or a large balance in my checking account. I can't possibly give you very much right now."

"That's fine. Write me a check for two thousand. You can go to the bank tomorrow and transfer funds if you need to. That will at least be a start. I'll be in touch to let you know where to send more."

"So you've made up your mind to not go back to Virginia?"

"I think it will be a long time before I can face that," she said. Slowly she got to her feet and braced herself carefully with both hands on the garden table.

"You don't look well. Surely, you don't plan to drive anywhere tonight."

Glenda couldn't believe she actually cared what happened to Elise. By all rights she shouldn't. Here was a woman who was blackmailing her and would have turned her over to the police if she had refused to play along. Elise was playing a dangerous game for sure, but no more dangerous than the one she was playing.

Only then did she begin to understand. Glenda suddenly saw another victim like herself as she looked at the pathetic woman across the table from her. The warm, motherly side of Glenda was beginning to take over again as the Valkyrie began to retreat.

Glenda picked up her checkbook and pen. "All right, I can do that, but don't come back here. Understand?"

"Don't worry. I'm certain you'll never see me again, but I'll be in touch." She watched closely as Glenda struck a match and lit the hurricane lamp on the table. When the check was written and signed, Elise took it quickly from Glenda's fingers, put it in her handbag, and tottered unsteadily out the garden gate. She heard the purr of the BMW as Elise sped away in the night.

Glenda quickly blew out the candle and sat in the garden for a long time, until the moon finally disappeared over the roof tops of the town. She would call in sick tomorrow, she decided. It was time this was all brought to an end. She would make sure that justice was done, but she had no doubt that the penance would be heavy.

When one repeats a tale told by a man,
He must report, as nearly as he can,
Every least word, if he remember it,
However rude it be, or how unfit;
Or else he may be telling what's untrue,
Embellishing and fictionizing too.
****

THE HOST
THE PROLOGUE OF THE CANTERBURY TALES
BY
GEOFFREY CHAUCER

Chapter 25

Late hours were beginning to take a toll on Dr. Emily, and the long meeting the night before with Sheriff Mitchell and Jess Thornton had left her feeling drained. Her usual early morning enthusiasm to start the day might improve with another cup of coffee, she thought, but she was not hopeful. She was up early and, with her exams completed, was ready to make her way across campus to her office and start thinking about preparations for the graduation ceremony which would take place in less than a week. Another shot of caffeine was all she needed to restore her energy, she thought, but she wasn't willing to take the time to brew another cup in her little French press coffee pot. She was counting on Glenda to share a cup of her morning coffee with her. Maybe that would be the boost she needed.

This had been the most difficult semester of Dr. Emily's entire career, but excellent news in her email that morning had gone a long way toward lifting her spirits. Jud Sharp had heard from her old alma mater, The University of Chicago, and would be receiving a fellowship which would just barely make it possible, with the help of a student loan, to move forward toward his life's ambition—the study of Anglo-Saxon and Medieval literature.

To say that Dr. Emily was proud of him was an understatement. She could have danced her way across campus if the worries that still plagued her could only be resolved. Instead, she found herself walking up the steps to Tutwiler Hall without the usual spring in her step. Slowly she made her way up the first flight of stairs to the English Department.

She paused at the office door of the department and thought it strange that Glenda was not at her desk. She was usually the first one to arrive in the morning. The light was blinking on the answer machine. Realizing the department was deserted, Dr. Emily took it upon herself to walk across to the desk and press the play button. Glenda must have overslept, she thought.

A familiar voice, one that Dr. Emily looked forward to hearing every morning greeted her. "Good morning, everyone. This is Glenda. I feel like I'm coming down with a little something. Nothing to worry about, I'm sure. Probably just the beginning of a pesky summer cold. Sorry to be out during this busy week, but I don't feel well enough to come to work today. I'm sure I'm contagious. I'll probably see you tomorrow."

Dr. Emily was disappointed. She had been counting on that coffee. Maybe one of the student assistants would show up soon and could be sent over to the Student Union to get her a cup. She wasn't going to take the time or effort this morning to rummage around in the office to brew a pot; besides she wasn't familiar with where Glenda kept the coffee supplies. The day was not off to a smooth start. Dr. Emily's mood plummeted.

She felt one of her mild migraine headaches coming on, no doubt from all the stress of the past few weeks. She had better take something for it. Of course, the caffeine in the coffee would have helped, but she was too impatient to wait for someone to show up and get a cup for her. Isn't it amazing, she thought, that when she wanted solitude there always seemed to be too many people around vying for her attention. Now that she needed just a little pampering, there was not a soul in sight. She reached in her purse and took out one of the prescription pills her doctor had given her for the occasional headache. She would have to make do with a sip of water from the fountain in the hall, she supposed. She remembered her doctor's cheerful words. "People with high IQs have a tendency to migraine headaches, Dr. Emily. You're in a select group." Then he had laughed. She wasn't amused in the least. What was so funny about that? Obviously he wasn't in that select group, or he wouldn't laugh about a migraine.

Finally, seated at her desk, she turned on her computer screen and logged into the campus software program that kept a record of the grades for her coursework. She would do one last check of her entries from yesterday since she had been so distracted and had found it difficult to focus on anything, especially on student grades or a computer program. After looking over her entries for a final time, she was satisfied that all was in order, and she allowed herself to sit quietly and think about the events of the day before.

Now that she had the time to reflect about the conversation with Jess and Kevin the previous evening, she was having second thoughts about one of her revelations. She wasn't sure if she should have mentioned the remark Glenda made the morning after

Jud's suicide attempt. Was there really any significance in Glenda saying anything about another suicide? It could very easily have been a recollection from the past, unrelated to the present case, something she had read about or seen on the news.

At times, Dr. Emily felt she had the unfortunate tendency to think out loud. She was certain that she had heard her correctly, but with Glenda out sick today there would be no opportunity to ask her about it again. Then there was the possibility that Glenda would remember nothing about her remark. After all, they had been so shocked and upset at Jud's suicide attempt; but there was still something about Glenda's reaction that continued to bother Dr. Emily.

The events of that morning when Jud was still in the hospital in a guarded condition kept replaying in her mind as she sat at her desk trying to think. Had Glenda seemed unwilling when she had asked her to repeat what she had said? Dr. Emily was certain she had heard her correctly, that she had made a comment about another suicide; but perhaps there was nothing to it. There had to be a reasonable explanation.

She felt certain Jess Thornton or Kevin Mitchell would make inquiries during the day and let her know if there had been any new developments in the case. There were still so many unanswered questions. And then there was that other curious matter. Was the fact that Glenda was from Virginia simply a coincidence? That was a reasonable assumption. After all, millions of people were from Virginia. Glenda couldn't possibly have anything to do with Basil Bowen's death. It was inconceivable.

The morning passed slowly for Dr. Emily as she sat at her desk thinking over the events of the last two months. A bee buzzed softly along the outside of the stately window in her office, and her head dropped slightly forward as she dozed off, but it was just for a moment. She quickly jerked herself awake. Having a migraine was no excused for sleeping in her office! She was horrified that this had happened at work, while she was sitting at her desk, no less; and she quickly turned to her computer screen and tried to think of a topic to research that would hold her attention.

I'm growing old, she realized. It was a bittersweet thought since it brought back memories of the past. She remembered her grandmother so well, sitting in her favorite chair in her parents' living room during family visits and High Holy Days. She would nod off, sitting straight up in her chair, just as Dr. Emily had done. She wouldn't sleep long, only dozing for a few minutes before she woke and tried to pretend she'd been following the conversation. The family would smile at each other, thinking it was amusing, and here I am doing the same thing, just like Grandmama.

This train of thought about her family led to reflection on her parents and her father in particular. This is what happens as we get older, she thought. We begin to reminisce about the past, and in some cases it becomes more real to us than the present. She must have dozed again for she could clearly see her dear father in his study turning the pages of a large book of botanical illustrations.

"There it is, Emily," he said. "A rather attractive plant for one so deadly, don't you think? Conium maculatum: a biennial herb with leaves like parsley—grows 3 to 6 feet tall—has many small white flowers in showy umbrels. All parts are poisonous, but the seeds are the most deadly. Found in North America in fields and along roadsides and in most other parts of the world, as well."

"Hemlock!" Dr. Emily was jolted back to the present. She stood up much too quickly from her desk and for a moment felt slightly lightheaded. Now where did I see hemlock growing, she asked herself. If it grows in fields and along roadsides, I've probably seen it no telling how many times and not recognized it. Now that I think about it I can almost see the illustration in my father's botany book. Small white flowers, leaves like parsley, and then she remembered. She remembered exactly where she had seen it.

Abruptly, Dr. Emily sat back down at her desk. What was the time? Close to eleven in the morning and she had dreamed almost the whole morning away. She almost wished she could start the whole day over again and not delve so deeply into who had poisoned Dr. Basil Bowen. Now that she had the answer, it was something she didn't want to face. Her heart was heavy, but she supposed there was no way to put off calling Jess Thornton and Sheriff Mitchell and telling them that she knew the identity of the murderer.

Before she called, however, she turned back to her computer screen and did a Google search on hemlock, just to double check the identification. Yes, there it was, just as she remembered it.

She picked up the phone on her desk and dialed Jess's mobile number.

"Jess," she said when he answered. "I know where the hemlock came from. I'm in my office. Let's not talk about it on the phone. Can you come right over?"

"I'm on my way, Dr. Emily."

Jess's reassuring voice helped some, but Dr. Emily was sick at heart and had an uneasy feeling.

While Dr. Emily had been conferring with Jess Thornton and Kevin Mitchell the night before, Glenda had spent the rest of the evening in her garden after Elise drove away. No matter where she goes, she will be easy to trace, Glenda thought. As soon as she cashes the check or uses a credit card, but she wasn't concerned in the least about what happened to Elise. She had several glasses of her favorite wine, but not too much. She knew she had to remain clearheaded.

She thought briefly about getting in her car and driving away herself. But where could she go? She knew it was inevitable that her true purpose for being at Merryvale College would soon be revealed. There was no point in trying to get away. If Elise had figured it out, the police wouldn't be far behind.

Yes, before long the police would discover that her nephew had been a protégé of Dr. Bowen's at the college in Virginia. All the sordid details would come to light, a story very similar to the one that almost took place on Merryvale campus. Her nephew had not been as strong minded as Jud; he was a sensitive, fragile boy still struggling with his identity as a homosexual. Jud, in comparison, had rejected Dr. Bowen's advances and was looking forward to a promising academic career. Jud, at least, had not been another sacrificial lamb, although he had come awfully close.

During the long night sitting in her garden trying to decide what to do, she thought a great deal about her own weaknesses. Her growing attachment to the people at Merryvale College and her love of the little cottage that had become her home had almost made her lose her resolve for revenge. The turning point had been the close call involving Jud. That had pushed her forward; that had made her act. She never imagined that she would be able to take another human life. But she felt justified; she had done it out of necessity, she told herself.

If only things had worked out differently. If only the truth about him had come out in Virginia instead of here, perhaps her nephew would still be alive. No point in going back to what might have been, she had no regrets. If she had done nothing to stop him, Basil Bowen would have continued to destroy lives, continued to prey on young men. In her own mind, she did what had to be done.

Now she must decide what she would do to put an end to the whole thing. She could go to the police and confess. Then she could tell them about Elise Bowen—that she had found out about the hemlock and was blackmailing her. There would be the check for two-thousand dollars deposited somewhere. They would catch up with her, Glenda had no doubt. If she took that course, Elise would have to face the music; but somehow, Glenda didn't think she would handle it that way. Elise Bowen, poor twisted soul, was just as much a victim as the rest of them. No, she wouldn't go to the police, she decided. As she had her entire life, she would do things her own way.

Well before daylight, Glenda went into the house and packed a few things in an overnight bag. After taking one more look around, she turned off the lights, went out the front door without bothering to lock it, and set off on foot down her street toward the campus.

The moon was very low now on the horizon. It must be getting fairly close to dawn, she thought. I'll have just enough time to make my way across campus without being seen. As she approached the Quad, the huge old trees blocked out the glimmer of the moon and she moved from shadow to shadow. At that early hour, there was no one about. She thought she would have just enough time.

In all this world there is no live creature
That's eaten or has drunk of this mixture
As much as equals but a grain of wheat,
That shall not sudden death thereafter meet...
****
THE PARDONER'S TALE
THE CANTERBURY TALES
BY
GEOFFREY CHAUCER

Chapter 26

By noon, Jess had met with Dr. Emily and listened intently as she told him about the hemlock growing along the back fence in Glenda's garden. She explained how she had praised Glenda on how nicely landscaped the garden was, and that she considered her a master gardener. She especially admired the background she had created with the taller plants, which she now realized was the hemlock, disguised in part by the graduated sizes of the smaller annuals growing in front and the fact it was not in bloom on her visits.

"You're sure that it's actually hemlock and not something else, Dr. Emily? I did a little reading up on it myself and found out it's easy to confuse with other plants like wild parsley." Jess still couldn't believe it.

"Yes, I'm certain, Jess. If only I had recognized it and made the connection before now. Of course, it probably wouldn't have saved Dr. Bowen's life. But then again, if I'd made some comment to her about how unusual it is to use hemlock as an ornamental it might have deterred her." Tears threatened to flow.

"I know how upsetting this must be to you, Dr. Emily; but you mustn't blame yourself. You had no idea that the hemlock would be used to poison the head of the department. Besides, you're a scholar of Anglo-Saxon and Medieval literature, not a botanist. You can't possibly think you could've changed the outcome of this tragedy. I guess I'll have to call Sheriff Mitchell, but I sure hate to. I know you're upset for Glenda's sake. Well, so am I. We've all grown pretty fond of her since she arrived on campus. Surely there's some explanation we're overlooking. There has to be! "

Jess was shaken by the news, but he was trying not to show it. As a professional, he had let himself become involved with someone too close to his job, and now had to face the consequences. He cared about Glenda and had been looking forward to the end of the investigation so he could continue to enjoy her company. Now that would never be possible, and he thought he must have been out of his mind to let himself get into this position. He supposed he would have to tell Kevin about their affair.

When Sheriff Mitchell arrived and got a clear account from Dr. Emily about the hemlock, he sadly confirmed that it was Glenda's nephew who had been involved with Dr. Bowen. The Sheriff's Department had just received the information from the police in Virginia. Now they had a suspect with a strong motive. Finally all the pieces were beginning to fit together, but they hated the way it looked for Glenda.

Sheriff Mitchell, with Jess Thornton in his role as campus police officer, requested a search warrant for Glenda's property, citing probable cause of finding a poison that had been instrumental in the death of Basil Bowen. All of this took up valuable time, but both men were intent on having procedures followed to the letter.

Because of their regard for her, they discussed the most tactful way of proceeding and considered calling Glenda and having her come in on the pretext of making an additional statement about a detail from the questioning on the day before. But in the end, they decided it would be best to wait for the search warrant and then go directly to her house. They had no reason to think she knew they had found out about her connection to the case; and since she had called in sick, they assumed that she was probably at home in bed. Although they wanted to question her as soon as possible, they didn't consider her a flight risk. They had no idea, of course, that Elise Bowen had paid her a visit the night before.

Both men felt they had time to proceed with established protocol. They would obtain the search warrant, drive to her house, and inform her of her rights. If she desired the representation of an attorney, she could call her own or be provided one by the court. At that time, with all legal bases covered, they would search her house and garden. Especially the garden. Little did they know that Glenda was hours ahead of them.

As they were leaving her office, Dr. Emily cautioned them to take great care in handling the hemlock. Contact with the skin and even breathing in bits of the leaves or pollen could cause severe respiratory distress and make them very ill. She suggested they contact an expert at one of the larger universities; Auburn would be a good choice, in order to take samples from the garden and then safely destroy the plants growing along Glenda's back garden fence.

The consequence of all of this discussion and deliberation was that much valuable time was lost in following the letter of the law. Midday had come and gone; and by the time a search warrant was obtained and an expert was contacted and had arrived on the scene, it was late afternoon.

Dr. Emily's office had somehow become the command post for the investigation; and although she knew she would be miserable if she were not involved, she longed for the peace of her little house. She just couldn't bring herself to leave. Jess Thornton finally got the ball rolling.

"Kevin, I'm about ready to get this over with!"

"I agree with you, Jess. Let's go to Glenda's house and present her with the search warrant and bring her in for questioning. I'll go ahead and take her in to the Sherriff's office, and you and the botany expert from Auburn go ahead and do the search. I would question her on campus, but maybe that might not be such a good idea. She has a lot of support here. It might be better to take her over to the Sheriff's Office, where proper procedure can't be in doubt. Also, I think it would cause the least embarrassment for everyone involved."

"Fine, I agree with you. I'll follow you and the botany professor over in my car," Jess said.

As they parked their cars in front of Glenda's house, Jess had the sinking feeling that they were already too late. He couldn't explain it, so he said nothing to them as they walked up to the front door and Kevin knocked. Jess was grateful he had not rung the bell. He didn't think he could handle hearing *Song of Joy.* The latch had not completely caught, and the door swung open at Kevin's sharp rap. Both men called out as they stepped gingerly into the little house, being careful not to touch anything, not certain if they were entering a crime scene or not. After a quick search inside, it was evident Glenda wasn't there.

The botanical expert, Dr. Michael Powell, had waited outside; but now Jess and Kevin took him around the side of the house and through the garden gate that Jess had entered so many times in the past. He halfway expected to find Glenda there since that was where she spent so much of her time, but the garden was empty. There was a forlorn look about it for some reason. An empty wine bottle and a fluted crystal glass sat on the garden table. They would be taken care of by forensics.

Jess and Kevin watched as Dr. Powell pulled on a pair of latex gloves and retrieved several plastic bags from his brief case. He put on a mask, the type worn by many people who have allergies to pollen, and lifted it slightly from over his mouth to speak to them before he started work.

"Yep, that's hemlock, all right. You have to be careful with this stuff. It looks very healthy. I'm going to take a few samples, and then I'll talk to you after I've cleaned up. Why don't you two go ahead and step out of the garden for a few minutes?"

Kevin and Jess looked at each other as if to say, is this guy for real? But they did as they were told and walked around the side of the house to the front yard.

"I've been in that garden a lot," Jess said, "and wasn't even aware I was that close to something so deadly."

"I think you have to have actual contact with the plant for it to cause you any problems," Kevin said. "I guess when you start taking cuttings from it, the cells of the plant are dispersed, and we could breathe them into our lungs."

"Lovely thought!" a shocked Jess said.

"Here he comes. He finished that pretty quick." Kevin remarked.

"I got all the samples I need for identification. I also took pictures of the plants, but I think it would be a good idea if your police photographer took some photos in a better light now that the sun's going down. Not that there's any question that it's hemlock. You just might want some good pictures for court. I'm going to leave an instruction sheet with you on proper disposal of the plants when your investigation is complete. As long as no one goes near them there should be no problem. I would secure the area though. We don't want curious kids getting in there."

"Thank you, Dr. Powell, for driving all this way and for helping us in our investigation. You realize you'll probably be called on to testify in court at some point," Kevin said.

"Certainly, I've done that many times. Always happy to help."

After Dr. Powell drove away, Jess turned to Kevin and said, "Now, what I want to know is where Glenda could have gone since her car is still parked in the garage."

"You and me both, buddy."

The broken slumbers and the sighing cold,
The sacred tears and the lamenting dire,
The fiery throbbing of the strong desire,
That all love's servants in this life endure...
****
THE KNIGHT'S TALE
THE CANTERBURY TALES
BY
GEOFFREY CHAUCER

Chapter 27

Although the days were beginning to lengthen, deep shadows were stretching their way across the Quad as Jess stopped by Dr. Emily's house around six that evening.

"Just checking on you," Jess said as Dr. Emily opened her front door in answer to his knock. "There's no sign of Glenda. Her car is in her garage, and there doesn't seem to be anything missing from her house. It doesn't look like she packed up her clothes or anything like that. I can't figure out where she could be, and I've got a bad feeling about it, Dr. Emily."

"I don't like it either, Jess. I'm very anxious, but Jud's coming over to spend the evening with me. I'm tired, but need the company. He said he would stay until I'm ready to go to bed. He has so many questions about the University of Chicago and wants to talk over his plans. Perhaps that'll take my mind off things for a while. But, Jess, the moment you hear anything, please let me know. I'm very worried about Glenda. I've grown very fond of her, you know."

"I will, although I don't think we'll find her tonight. She must have had almost the whole day to slip away. I just can't figure out why she didn't take her car. She's smart though. She knew we would have alerted all the authorities to be on the lookout for her."

"Thank you so much for stopping by. I know you'll let me know as soon as you hear anything. You look exhausted yourself. Why don't you go home and try to get some sleep. I doubt there's much more you can do tonight."

"Thanks, Dr. Emily. I think I'll do that."

As Jess pointed his car toward home, he waved at Jud as he passed him walking up the sidewalk toward Dr. Emily's house. I'm glad those two have found each other, he thought. He's like a son to her and will probably always be a part of her life. Two kindred spirits. That's about the only good thing I can think of that's come out of all of this.

When he arrived at his small apartment, he put a microwave dinner in the oven and switched on the television. Eating in front of the television was not one of Jess's favorite things, but tonight he was just too tired to go out for dinner or to cruise over to the campus cafeteria. He stretched out on the sofa, and before long he was sound asleep.

He wasn't sure what woke him up. His sofa was pretty miserable to sleep on, and it didn't help that he'd fallen asleep fully dressed without even taking off his shoes. Once awake, however, Jess had no desire to undress and go back to sleep in his bed. Besides being stiff and sore, he had an unsettled feeling, a restlessness that he couldn't seem to shake. He rubbed his eyes and ran his fingers through his hair. Slowly he massaged his temples trying to get rid of the mild headache that had bothered him for most of the past twenty-four hours. Tension, he guessed. He might as well go back to campus and make sure everything was okay. He looked at his watch—3:30 a.m. It should be quiet at this hour, but he still felt uneasy.

Back in his patrol car he cruised toward campus and through the main gate. Directly across the Quad was Main Hall. The darkness of the grounds was only slightly illuminated by a few dim lights placed here and there along the brick walks. The waning full moon from the night before had already moved below the roof tops of the town and gave off only a faint glow. It was those few hours before sunrise that would always stay with

Jess in future years when he thought about the events that were about to unfold, when the final chapter would be written in one of the most painful episodes of his life.

He drove his patrol car slowly around the campus, taking his time as he took in as much as he could in the darkness. All was quiet. He drove out to the college lake and shone his flashlight across the dark water and thought perhaps tomorrow they should send out a team to search the lake area. He was sure Glenda had not gone very far, and he feared the worst.

He left the lake and drove back to the main gate. He stopped at the small guardhouse that was manned by campus police twenty-four hours a day, in hopes that it had been a quiet night. The eleven-seven shift was one of the roughest, with rowdy students causing trouble at the beginning and then the struggle to stay awake during the early morning hours when all was so unearthly still, just as it was now. It must be almost four in the morning, he thought, as he stepped out of his car. Hal Henderson, the night duty officer, came outside to greet him.

"Seems pretty quiet, Hal. Easy night?"

"Not bad. Some of the frat boys whooped it up a little around midnight. I let them off with a warning. After all, it's almost the end of the semester; so I guess they needed to blow off a little steam. Why are you up so early?"

"I don't know. Just a feeling I guess."

They stood there in companionable silence for a few minutes. Jess thought he heard on owl hoot somewhere nearby. The maintenance people waged a continuous battle trying to keep all sorts of birds from nesting in the attics of several of the old buildings on campus. Jess remembered once, when workmen had been renovating Main Hall, they had disturbed a large owl during the daylight hours. It had flown down to the ground, helpless, blinded by the sun until it was rescued by one of the biology professors and kept safe until it could be relocated. He told Hal about the owl.

Talking about the owl had made him glance across the Quad to Main Hall. The largest and second oldest building on campus, it was built solidly out of red brick that had faded over the years to a deep rose. Wisteria wound around the stone arches that graced the front portico.

"Let's walk over toward Main," he said to Hal.

As they walked across the thick carpet of grass, Jess looked up at the dark windows of the building. None of the girls seemed to be up pulling an all-nighter studying for finals, he mused. His eyes traveled up to the fourth floor; and then, with a shock, he saw a light burning in one of the two rooms directly above the top floor of the dorm, built there like an afterthought, as if the architect had decided to add a penthouse or a suite on top of his creation.

These were the two rooms that formed the basis of all those old ghost stories about girls who had died there and whose spirits still haunted the place. Many years before, the rooms had been closed off; and not one student for as long as anyone could remember had lived there. A few girls had moved in briefly over the years, no one could say exactly when, but quickly moved out; and so the legend grew year after year as the stories were told and retold to incoming freshmen.

"Must be the ghost," said Hal.

"That's no ghost," Jess snapped.

"Well, it does happen, as strange as it might seem. I can't tell you how many times I've been up there with scared girls hanging on to the back of my shirt to find absolutely nothing. Yeah, the light would be on. I would turn it off, and down we would all come until it happened again. Just someone playing a joke, I guess. But I'll be the first to admit it's kind of creepy up there. Feels cold, even on the hottest night."

"You haven't made your last trip. Get out your keys. You're going up there again, and I'm going with you this time."

Slowly and as quietly as they could, Jess and Hal made their way up the four flights of stairs, avoiding the noisy elevator. It was a broad staircase with beautifully carved bannisters and newel posts, but on the fourth floor the staircase ended in a large landing identical to those below.

Directly opposite the stairs was a single door that was always kept locked, and behind that door was a narrow set of steps that went up to the rooms above. All of the ghost stories revolved around these two rooms. The college had long ago given up assigning them to any of the students. It would have been considered cruel and unusual punishment. Hal inserted his key and opened the door.

"Since we saw the light from the outside, it has to be coming from up here," Hal whispered. He walked along the narrow passage at the top of the steps and opened the door to the left. Nothing but darkness, with a faint glow from the window. He shone his flashlight around the room. "Empty, as usual," he said.

"Give me the key," Jess said as he turned from the empty room. As he approached the remaining door, Jess felt the sweat break out on his body. He inserted the key and stepped inside the dimly lit space. His first instinct was to look up at the weak bulb hanging from the ceiling, then across to the window that looked out on the Quad. Then he shone his flashlight across the floor.

Hal looked over Jess's shoulder. "Oh, my god!" he exclaimed.

"Don't come in Hal," Jess said. "Forensics will need to go over everything, and we don't want to destroy any evidence."

Jess walked on tiptoe to the side of the body and leaned down to check for a pulse although he could tell it was much too late. She had probably been dead for several hours, he thought. He stood completely still as he tried to take in everything in the room. There was a small suitcase with soft sides, no more than an overnight bag, flung into a corner of the room. Candles were arranged in a semi-circle around the lower portion of the body. Some were still burning; others had burned the wick totally down and been extinguished.

Crouching down as close to the body as he could get, he examined every last detail. Glenda lay on what appeared to be the cape she had worn as the Wife of Bath. It was a heavy, full-cut garment, carefully spread out, and served as a pallet for her body to rest on instead of the bare wooden floor. She was dressed in most of her original costume as the Wife of Bath. She even wore her bright red stockings and the well-cut dress with the overskirt. Only the wimple and the wide hat were missing.

Lying on the left side of her body at the edge of her cape, there appeared to be a full confession written in her hand and signed. Jess leaned over and read it without picking it up. In a brief, simply-worded statement she described the murder of Dr. Basil Bowen. Using the hemlock from her garden, she had placed the poison that she had processed herself in a flask mixed with brandy. She had given him the drink early on the morning of the Faire as he was preparing to mount up for his ride to the Quad. He had seemed ill and she held his arm. Although he had one of his own, when she gave him the flask he drank its entire contents and handed it back to her. It contained more than enough hemlock to kill him. She went on to explain why she was driven to murder and, in closing, revealed that Elise Bowen had seen her give Basil the flask and was blackmailing her. Near her right hand was what appeared to be an empty container of prescription medication along with an empty wine bottle.

Jess covered his eyes with his hand for a moment as he looked down at her. He had not loved her, but he had cared for her and enjoyed her company. He couldn't believe what he was seeing; but, although he was shaken, he regained control of his emotions. It was then that he noticed one thing he had missed in his initial examination. At her feet inside the semi-circle of candles was a small piece of paper. Leaning over for a closer look, Jess saw that Glenda had written the last two lines of the description of the Wife of Bath:

The remedies of love she knew, perchance,
For of that art she'd learned the old, old dance.

****

Below this inscription was a final message that must have been written later as the wine and the pills had begun to take effect. Her writing had become unsteady and spidery.

For my nephew, Austin

Amor vincit Omnia.
(Love conquers all)

You go to Canterbury; may god speed
And the blest martyr soon requite your meed.
****
THE HOST
THE PROLOGUE OF THE CANTERBURY TALES
BY
GEOFFREY CHAUCER

Chapter 28

The graduating class of Merryvale College held their diplomas in one hand and tossed their caps high into the air with a resounding shout of joy! As she did every year, Dr. Emily hosted a small group of friends at her home after the ceremony. During the festivities, she slipped away from her guests just long enough to meet with Sheriff Mitchell and Jess Thornton in the privacy of her office with the door firmly shut. Since the night when Glenda's body was discovered, they had had very little time to talk over the tragic events that had rocked the campus.

"You both realize, I'm sure, that I want my part in the solving of this crime to be kept as secret as possible;

and I want to thank you ahead of time for your professional handling of this case and for your discretion. Both of you must know how much I value your friendship. However, there are just a few things I was wondering about."

"Of course, Dr. Emily, what do you want to know?" Jess asked.

"How did Glenda get across campus, into Main Hall, and unlock the door to the upper rooms without being seen?"

"I think I can answer that," Kevin replied. "The locks on those two rooms at the top of Main Hall can be opened with a paper clip. Seriously, if you know what you are doing, you could probably unlock anything on this campus. As far as getting into the dorm is concerned, people respond to the familiar. Glenda was known to almost everyone on campus as an employee of the college. Probably someone opened the door for her if it was too early for the main doors to be unlocked from the outside. We're asking questions about that right now; but so far no one has admitted to letting her in, and I doubt they ever will."

"Just one last question before I rejoin my guests and fulfill my duties as a hostess. Didn't Dr. Bowen have a flask with him? I believe several people commented on seeing him with one?"

"You're right, Dr. Emily," Kevin replied. "The flask Dr. Bowen was carrying was with his belongings when he was brought to the ER. Of course, those items were returned to Elise after his death. But once we knew we had a murder on our hands, his clothes and personal items were impounded. Elise had put the flask away in a cabinet and she had returned his costume to the Drama Department. We lost a lot of valuable time looking for that flask. Eventually everything was turned over to forensics, but there wasn't a trace of anything in it except alcohol. All of the poison must have come from Glenda's flask, but we can't locate it in her house. There's been a lot of confusion about those two flasks. One belonged to Dr. Bowen and the other one was Glenda's. It seems he drank from both. I'm sure she must have disposed of hers somewhere. Without that written confession, we might still be looking for the murderer. You know, this would have been a really difficult case to bring to trial. It's possible she might have gotten away with it."

Dr. Emily's blue eyes filled with tears. "You both know I cared about her. I think in time we would have become close friends, but I understand how she must have felt and what drove her to take another person's life. Not that I condone violence, but it's an old, old story. From early Greek mythology to the present day, writers have tried to explain the psychology of the individual seeking revenge. Well, it's over now. I hope she will rest in peace."

"We all do," Jess said softly.

"Yes," Kevin said, "It truly is over. Oxford will pursue the question of identity theft and improve their security, I'm sure. Something we should probably do as well. Also the police in England think that our guy, our phony Basil, was a distant relative. I suppose he somehow got access to the deceased's records. It's probably as simple as having his password; but, really, what does it matter now? The man is dead. End of story. As for Elise Bowen, the police will catch up with her before long. She's a beautiful woman driving a highly recognizable car. I don't believe she will get very far; and when they find her, she'll be facing a blackmail charge. At least, there should be enough evidence to convict her."

Dr. Emily left the two men to talk in her study and circulated through the house, making sure all of her guests were enjoying themselves and the celebration of another graduation. Max followed her every step, his tail wagging, never taking his eyes off his mistress.

"I think Max is actually enjoying himself this evening," she said to a group of her friends. "He doesn't enjoy parties very much and makes himself scarce, usually under my bed or the sideboard in the dining room. Scotties tend to be a little standoffish, as most of you know who've tried to make friends with him. But lately he has developed a strong bond with Jud, I'm happy to report. I believe he'll miss him when he leaves for the University of Chicago."

All of her guests expressed happiness for Jud and for her. They knew how pleased she was that he would be attending her alma mater and how fond she was of her protégé. It was an evening for celebration and not one to dwell on the tragedy that had marred the end of the school year. She would enjoy herself too, she decided, and celebrate with her friends; and as Glenda had said that last night in her garden, "All debts have been paid in full!"

About the Author

Sharon Freeman Laborde has had a long and rewarding career in public education in both rural and inner city high schools. The mother of two grown children, she divides her time between her homes in Alabama and Arkansas where she is active in environmental issues, organic gardening and the arts.